# SPECIAL MESSAGE TO READERS

**THE ULVERSCROFT FOUNDATION**
**(registered UK charity number 264873)**
was established in 1972 to provide funds for
earch, diagnosis and treatment of eye diseases.
Examples of major projects funded by
the Ulverscroft Foundation are:-

- The Children's Eye Unit at Moorfields Eye Hospital, London
- The Ulverscroft Children's Eye Unit at Great Ormond Street Hospital for Sick Children
- Funding research into eye diseases and treatment at the Department of Ophthalmology, University of Leicester
- The Ulverscroft Vision Research Group, Institute of Child Health
- Twin operating theatres at the Western Ophthalmic Hospital, London
- The Chair of Ophthalmology at the Royal Australian College of Ophthalmologists

can help further the work of the Foundation
by making a donation or leaving a legacy.
ery contribution is gratefully received. If you
uld like to help support the Foundation or
quire further information, please contact:

**THE ULVERSCROFT FOUNDATION**
**The Green, Bradgate Road, Anstey**
**Leicester LE7 7FU, England**
**Tel: (0116) 236 4325**

website: ' t.com

R.S. Hill was born and grew up in North Devon. He taught English as a Foreign Language in Greece before becoming Head of Department in a comprehensive school and, later, a local authority consultant. He now writes full-time. Hill has contributed articles on travel, local history and educational subjects to various magazines and newspapers.

# THE RESCUER

Bideford, 1873: The River Torridge is in flood. Almost as soon as she sets foot in the town, Abigail March saves a young woman from drowning. The daughter of a progressive Canadian politician, Abigail is here on official business, standing in for her father. Accompanied by Inspector Theodore Newton of the Metropolitan Police, she has travelled to Devonshire to inspect a captured shipment of firearms being guarded by the local police. That night, the woman she saved is murdered. Then the weapons are found to have disappeared. A man is arrested — but when Abigail befriends the brother of the accused, she and Newton believe a potentially tragic mistake has been made . . .

R. S. HILL

---◆---

# THE
# RESCUER

*Complete and Unabridged*

# ULVERSCROFT
*Leicester*

First published in Great Britain in 2015 by
Robert Hale Limited
London


First Large Print Edition
published 2016
by arrangement with
Robert Hale Limited
London

A catalogue record for this book is available
from the British Library.

ISBN 978–1–4448–2941–9


Published by
F. A. Thorpe (Publishing)
Anstey, Leicestershire

Set by Words & Graphics Ltd.
Anstey, Leicestershire
Printed and bound in Great Britain by
T. J. International Ltd., Padstow, Cornwall

This book is printed on acid-free paper

*For Val*

# 1

There was a woman in the river.

Along the quay, everyone was shouting. Fishermen flung down their nets; crewmen scrambled up through the hatches; shipwrights dropped their tools. The tide was the highest it had been all spring. Carriage drivers reined back their nags; drinkers tumbled out through the doorway of the Newfoundland Inn; a boy who had been idly staring at seagulls pointed in horror. On the bridge, horses shied and carts skewed; shocked pedestrians craned over the parapet.

She looked like a mushroom bobbing on its cap in a kitchen sink. Her brown travelling skirt ballooned under her; clad in a silk blouse, her torso stuck up like a stalk. Her hair collapsed in hanks over her shoulders even though her hat remained precariously pinned. As she battled to make swimming strokes against the current, the tide spirited her past the vessels moored up and down the quay, waltzed her midstream and swung her on a fairground ride towards the glassy whirlpools under the arches of the stone bridge.

Then the onlookers saw that there was someone else.

So the woman had not lost her footing on the edge of the quay, nor was this some desperate attempt at suicide: she was a rescuer. As she beat her arms against the water, shouts of alarm turned to cheers. Right before their eyes, the onlookers witnessed her snatch the other body from the whirligig tide, hook her arm around it and strike out.

By this time, a fisherman from one of the smacks had loosened a rowing dinghy. But before he could climb aboard, the current spun the boat like a leaf out into the centre of the river. The local men shouted to each other not to jump in. They respected the ebb and flow of the tides; from childhood, they had grown up with stories of capsizings and death by water. People still talked about the day the horse-drawn omnibus bound for Torrington fair tipped off the quay and eight souls were lost. Everyone knew a swimmer had no chance of making headway; the only hope was to try to stay afloat. They all understood the treachery of the whirlpools under the bridge where the surface looked as smooth as a mirror, but the current towed so hard underneath that nothing could escape being pulled down.

By now most of the town had lined the quay. All up the High Street, shops emptied; people raced from under the trees at the far end of the quay. On the opposite bank, shipwrights from the repair yard downed tools and charged across the bridge. Some young idiot got his friends to lower him by his ankles over the parapet; he reached down to the surface of the water hoping to catch the woman if the tide should sweep her his way. He hung suspended until his friends could hold him no longer and heaved him back up.

All this time, the current lurched the woman this way and that. Her skirts, which a few minutes previously buoyed her up, now dragged her down. She was tiring. Her head was barely above the surface; her hat had gone; she gulped air like a landed fish. With one arm, she made half-hearted strokes to try to gain control, but the current teased her with a spin towards the quay and then swung her midstream again.

But still she clung on to the body. At least, the crowds along the quay presumed it was a body. All they could see was a mat of black hair flung like bladderwrack over the face. No one believed that whoever it was could be alive. As everyone roared encouragement, arguments broke out as to who the rescuer might be; no one recognized her. As it was not unusual for the smaller smacks to be crewed by a fisherman and his wife, the crowd presumed she had come in on one of the boats. That was who she was, they decided; no one with local knowledge would have dreamed of taking on the undertow. But as to who the poor wretch she had thrown herself in to save was, they had no idea.

Recent storms and a flood tide meant that every mooring along the quay was taken while the skippers waited for a break in the weather. At the far end, where the river turned and widened into the estuary, craft were lashed two and three abreast. Here, in the lee of the town, there was shelter from the wind; round the headland beyond the sand bar, Atlantic gales raged.

As the two bodies swirled back and forth, men from a full-rigged brig lowered a second dinghy. The first was now jammed against the bridge where the water nearly touched the top of the arches. The men were more cautious this time. Three of them lay belly down on the deck and held the craft tight to the side while two more men climbed over them to board. One had ropes and boathooks and the other took care with the oars; they knew what they were doing. Ignoring the plentiful advice and instructions shouted at them from the quayside, they concentrated on shoving themselves out into the current. Almost at once, the boat lurched side-on out of the oarsman's control. He fought to pull it round. Midstream, the two bodies were just visible.

The woman had stopped trying to swim towards the bank now. From what the onlookers on the bridge could tell, she concentrated on kicking with her legs to keep both their heads above the surface and when her legs tired, she struck out with her arm. The current held her and whoever it was she was holding up.

Conversation in the crowd turned to the length of time they had been in the water. Five minutes, ten; they must be freezing. They talked about how the woman's legs must be stiffening up under the surface; how numbness must be overtaking her; how the cold could make her slip into unconsciousness; how deceptive the strength of these spring tides was and how futile it was to try and fight them.

Despite the oarsman's best efforts, one line of current pirouetted the dinghy towards a slipway on the far bank; at the same time, another propelled the bodies towards the quay. The crowd roared encouragement as more men leaned over the gunwales of the sloops moored nearest the bridge. Another young fisherman was held by his legs, as the bodies swirled close. The woman in the water came to enough to realize where the current was taking her and raised her arm. As the young man made a grab for her, the crowd erupted.

Practically in the water himself, the man struggled to get a secure grip. He was shouting instructions to her, but no one could hear because of the uproar from the bridge. Somehow he managed to fasten both hands on her forearm and pull her towards him. The crowd could see the woman's desperate face. She still had her other arm locked across the chest of whoever it was she had thrown herself in to save. Men from the quay jumped down on to the deck and leaned out to where the woman was being held; their arms stretched straight out like a line of oars. They shouted encouragement; they grabbed for her wrist. The agony of having her arm wrenched almost out of its socket was etched on the woman's face; the current swung her body dangerously towards the bridge and its whirlpools.

Then, just as more men desperate to help clambered on to the deck of the sloop, the fisherman lost her. The woman's wet arm slid through his grip; her face dissolved in horror as she felt the tug of the current. She stared up at the fisherman; her hand pawed the air, fingers outstretched towards him. As she slipped free, the brown water closed over her head.

On the bridge, there was mayhem. Women screamed; men rained abuse on the young fisherman who hung over the side of his boat now, desperately combing the water with his arms. Some of the other men on the deck leaned over him to rake the surface of the river with their boathooks. Everyone was convinced the woman was lost; onlookers crossed to the other side of the bridge expecting to see corpses borne by the current under one of the arches. Eventually, the noise died; silent dismay gripped everyone as they stared at the surface of the muddy water which fitted as tight as a coffin lid.

A second after the shock of witnessing this horror, there was a bellow like a wounded bull from the back of the crowd; a man screamed a woman's name and cannoned through. Disorientated by what he saw, he was distraught; his helplessness made him rage. Obviously used to being in command and having orders obeyed, he yelled for people to get out of his way. His cry tore at his throat.

'Abigail, Miss March.'

No one on the quay knew who the man

was. He was tall, about thirty; his new London suit and brown boots looked out of place. His side whiskers were neatly shaved; he had an open face, high forehead and the solid shoulders of a military man. As he scrambled on to the deck of the fishing boat, he tore at the buttons of his jacket and yanked his arms out of the sleeves. He hopped first on one leg then the other to pull off his boots, then barged through the line of men with boathooks. The quayside crowd gasped: the man was determined to throw himself in. They shouted to the men on the deck to stop him; a couple of fishermen seized his arms.

Just as the man wrestled himself free, there was a roar from the bridge. The woman's head broke the surface; she gasped for air just below the prow of the next boat upstream. A line trailed over the side and she grabbed it.

Immediately, men leapt from the quay, hurled themselves across the deck, leaned down, grabbed the woman and held her. Her arm was still locked around the body. As the men lifted her by the shoulders, then the waist and slowly heaved the two of them on to the deck of the boat, the cry went up from the bridge that the second body was also a woman. Because of the sorry state of her cotton dress, her sodden hair across her face and the commotion going on around her, no one had been able to recognize her.

'Miss March, Abigail,' called the tall man.

He had shoved through the crowd and now stood in shirtsleeves and bare feet beside the two women. He crouched down, ordered the crowd to stand back, turned the bodies on to their sides and watched the women vomit gutfuls of river water on to the deck, cough, gasp, gulp, fight for air and struggle to come to. They pushed themselves up on to their elbows in an effort to rid themselves of the water in their lungs, hawked and spat out the taste of the river. After the foul water, the air burned their throats and they coughed convulsively.

The crowd was gleeful. They shouted encouragement, laughed with relief, teased the women with jokes about their not needing a drink for a while. The two women were still putty-faced and shook with cold; they seemed oblivious to everything except the feeling of the hard wooden deck on which they lay.

'Blankets,' called the man in shirtsleeves, staring angrily round at the crowd.

A minute later Lizzie Hookway, landlady of the Newfoundland Inn across the quay, strong-armed her way through, and lobbed two grey blankets down on to the deck. She was short and broad-shouldered; her hair was

9

pushed up under a mobcap and she had a wide, kindly face. With sleeves rolled up and her arms and apron covered in flour, she looked every inch the competent manager, used to taking charge whenever there was trouble. She stood with her hands on her hips and assessed the situation. As the women pulled the coverings round themselves, she called out for them to be brought across to revive themselves in front of a fire.

Most of the crowd seemed to consider heading in the direction of the Newfoundland Inn after that. Conversation took a philosophical turn as everyone reflected on the nature of luck, human courage and the possibility of divine intervention. As they stared at the two half-drowned women and the stranger kneeling over them in his shirtsleeves, there was just one question in the minds of the onlookers: who were they?

*Half an hour earlier*

When the mid-afternoon train pulled into the new Bideford station at East-the-Water, all three carriages were full. The livery paintwork of the engine gleamed glossy maroon; the funnel shone black and the brass dome and safety valve were polished as bright as sunlight. The letters L.S.W.R. were picked out in proud gold capitals along the side. Steam exploded from under the wheels. The driver leaned out of his cab and watched the porter unload the guard's van.

The stationmaster, George Westcott, took up a position by the exit and kept an eye on the steel pocket watch which lay in the palm of his hand. He was a short, dumpy man; his florid cheeks were framed by wiry mutton chops; his uniform cap was squarely on his head. When he was satisfied with his time-check, he gave the driver an approving nod just to show who was in charge, slipped the watch into a waistcoat pocket, tucked in his thumbs and leaned slightly backwards to counter-balance the weight of his stomach.

Passengers disembarked in a hurry. Knowing there would not be enough places for everyone, they made a beeline for the horse-drawn coaches which stood outside in the station yard waiting to ferry them across the bridge into town. Some of them stood back to allow a woman carrying an infant in her arms to leave ahead of them. The woman wore a long, dark coat; a black veil hung from her hat and hid her face. She spoke to no one. The station porter hurried after her carrying her valise.

After the crowd had dispersed, another

woman and two men were left on the platform; the porter returned to deal with their luggage. This woman was in her twenties, confident and sharp-eyed, with her hair piled under a striking, wide-brimmed hat decorated with a peacock feather that drew lines in the air each time she turned her head. She wore a brown tailored travelling jacket over a pearl blouse. Her skirt was in the same expensive fabric as the jacket, cut over a modest tournure to provide a slim, modern silhouette; it ended an inch or two above the ground for ease of walking. At every step the woman took, there was a flash of black-laced, red-silk boots and the click of fashionable, military heels. Clearly delighted to have arrived, she was anxious not to miss anything and strode up the platform ahead of the men.

The station was built into the hillside almost directly over the old stone bridge. From the end of the platform, the view was over the river and the town whose houses huddled tightly together across the opposite hillside. Pale, lime-washed walls were golden in the afternoon sun; open casements glittered where they caught the light; smoke from terracotta chimney-pots curled up over the black slate roofs.

At the end of the bridge, a grand civic building caught the young woman's eye; a square church tower with its white-faced clock pushed up from amidst the crowd of rooftops. Along the quay, boats rode high in the water: ketches, smacks, sloops, barques, a brigantine, some square-rigged, some fore and aft, were moored two and three abreast. A forest of masts, gaffs and spars swayed above them. One vessel's mast, she noticed, was broken and trailed in the water alongside her. The river ran fast; sand from the estuary churned with river mud and made the water as brown as old shoe leather. The incoming tide was almost on the turn.

At the far end of the station platform away from the stink of smoke and engine oil, the afternoon air smelled of the sea. Beside the station house, a bed of vivid daffodils nodded their trumpets towards the sun. White clouds raced across a blue sky; the wind blew hard from the south-west.

Below the station, downstream of the bridge, a ketch was dry-docked for repair; a few yards further on, a coaster was being loaded with ball clay. The bridge itself was busy with afternoon traffic. The carriages from the station had almost reached the quay; an unsteady cyclist wove along on an ancient boneshaker behind a carrier's cart.

One of the men who had just disembarked took charge.

'Miss March, we'll wait here for a carriage to take us to our hotel.'

Inspector Theodore Newton stood tall and square-shouldered rather as if he were on parade. He wore a new-looking, fawn-coloured suit, a brown bowler and carried a rolled copy of yesterday's *Times*. He called up the platform with a note of authority in his voice, yet when the woman turned back to answer him, a blush crept above his collar.

'Nonsense.' The woman laughed. 'A walk would do us all good. It's a beautiful afternoon. We've been sitting like chickens in a coop box for hours.'

'Well . . . ' Newton was too gentlemanly to contradict her.

'We'd all like that, wouldn't we?' the woman continued pleasantly. 'And I've told you, Inspector, it's Abigail, please.'

She smiled warmly at him and gestured with her arm.

'This view. What a wonderful place.'

Westcott peered at the woman. No one ever wanted to walk. Of all the passengers he'd seen disembark, he'd never encountered anyone quite like her, with her confidence, her red boots and strange accent which he couldn't recognize. A bit above herself, he decided; he whispered a suggestion to make it easy for the men.

'I'll send Norman,' he confided to Newton, 'for a carriage.'

Before he could answer, he bellowed, 'Norman' at no one in particular.

A second later, a thin, pale boy, about twelve years old, appeared from the main door to the station house, broom in hand. He wore a patched shirt, a pair of hand-me-down trousers with twine for a belt, a cap rammed down over his eyes and boots that were scuffed and split.

'What?' Norman squinted into the sunlight.

'You've just picked up that broom, haven't you?'

Norman stared defiantly.

'Carriage,' Westcott said firmly.

Norman tutted, rolled his eyes and dropped his shoulders in resignation.

'Now.' Westcott glared at him. He nodded to indicate the man standing next to him.

The boy turned and plodded into the station house, suddenly stooped as though someone had loaded a pack on his back. Minutes later, Abigail saw him, hands sunk in his pockets, trudge across the bridge towards town.

'That's considerate of you.' Abigail beamed at Westcott. 'But it's a sunny day, we should stretch our legs. I'll go on ahead.'

15

'We can't have you walking on your own.' Newton sounded alarmed.

'I assure you I'm quite capable of it,' Abigail laughed.

'I merely meant . . . ' Words collapsed in Newton's mouth. 'I'll accompany you. Sergeant Culley can wait here and come on with the luggage.'

Newton should have known better. The journey down from London had been instructive. By the time they reached Reading, Newton had learned that Miss March could wrong-foot him if she wished; as the Wiltshire fields rolled by he realized he was dealing with someone whose will was at least as strong as his own; by the time the train pulled into Exeter he understood that despite her charm and cheerful manner, she would flat-out contradict him if she felt like it. Suddenly aware that his new suit had become crumpled by hours of sitting in a railway carriage, Newton did his best to smooth the creases out of the sleeves of his jacket with the palm of his hand.

'Surely . . . ' Abigail turned to the sergeant.

'I'll be fine, ma'am.' Culley smiled. 'Best that someone stays with the luggage.'

Culley wore a dark serge suit, dusty from the journey and shiny at the elbows. He was in his twenties, lean, wiry and strong. He had dark side whiskers and the crow's feet at the corners of his eyes made him look older than his years; his nose had been broken some time ago.

'You won't have long to wait.' Westcott clarified. 'Fifteen minutes and the carriage will be back here and loaded up, if Norman don't dawdle.'

Inspector and sergeant, Westcott's ears had pricked up at the mention of the ranks. Not local, that was for sure; come up from Exeter most likely. And that woman didn't seem to be with either of them. Maybe he would find out more from the sergeant after the other two had gone.

Abigail turned abruptly and headed through the station building, calling pleasantly for Newton to follow her. A few minutes later, having negotiated the downhill bend of Station Road, they were on the bridge with the town in front of them. As he fell in with Abigail's pace, Newton was surprised by how quickly she walked. Halfway across, Abigail pointed out the ketch with the broken mast.

'Must be the one,' Newton agreed. 'In a sorry state by the look of her.'

Abigail's heels click-clicked. Flashes of red darted out from under her skirt like tongues. Newton couldn't take his eyes off them.

'A very fine pair of boots,' Newton said

stiffly. 'If you don't mind my saying so.'

'I think everyone should treat themselves to a pair of red boots; even you, Inspector.' Abigail enjoyed teasing him; she discovered he had no defences against it. 'Then we would all feel good and the world would be a better place.'

Newton privately congratulated himself on having invested in a new suit. Under normal circumstances he rarely gave his clothes a second thought, but a week ago he would never have dreamed he would be taking the Devonshire air with a fashionable young woman beside him. He just hoped he would be able to get by with wearing the new suit for the duration of the stay and wouldn't have to resort to his threadbare old suit which was currently inexpertly folded in his leather suitcase back at the station.

'Papa sent me out shopping the day we arrived in London.' Abigail's enthusiasm was infectious. 'My sisters will be so jealous. Fashions here are months ahead of what we get back home; these boots are straight from Paris.'

Newton pointed out Tanton's Hotel on the quay where rooms had been booked for the three of them. To Newton's relief, it looked solidly respectable; he hoped Abigail would approve. Anyway, it was only a short stay. His police duties were straightforward and if the Borough Superintendent had done his job properly, all three of them should be back on the train to London in a day or two at the outside.

'Aren't you glad we walked?' Abigail turned to him. 'Poor Sergeant Culley, you should have let him come too.'

Newton smiled at the young woman's forwardness.

'No need to worry about Culley,' he assured her.

'The importance of exercise is not widely appreciated,' Abigail went on. 'I learned that during my medical studies. Bicycling would be my preference, though. Back home in Nova Scotia they are building velocipede rinks; by the end of this year we shall have five in Halifax alone. It is the most wonderful fun. The exhaustion you feel afterwards is quite exhilarating.'

She guessed that Newton would find this shocking.

'I have never bicycled,' Newton said stiffly.

'The rinks make it much easier,' Abigail went on. 'Our road surfaces are impossible.'

'So you ride round in circles, is that it?' Newton was determined to sound unimpressed.

'Round the perimeter, anywhere really.' Abigail smiled.

Newton held back from commenting that this seemed to him utterly pointless and smiled at her in return.

'Walking is also excellent exercise,' Abigail went on innocently. 'Swimming is best of all for the constitution. My father is a keen swimmer and made sure all we girls knew how to swim.'

Newton stared directly ahead and did not rise to the bait.

As they reached the town end of the bridge, the traffic swelled. Crates, nets and coils of rope cluttered the quayside. The air smelled of tar from the rigging and fish. Children played amongst the mooring ropes. With deft movements of their shuttles, fishermen worked on their nets; pedestrians dodged between farm carts and riders. A line of grey-whiskered men with clay pipes in their hands sat on benches outside the bay windows of the Newfoundland Inn. On a flat piece of ground, a gang of dirty-faced children was engrossed in a marbles game. Close by, an older boy sat on a mooring bollard and stared up at the wheeling gulls. Newton spotted Norman a short distance away. With his eyes glued on the gutter, he walked slowly up and down as if he were searching for something. A pair of carriages for hire stood idle at the top of one of the slipways.

'Culley will be waiting all night.' Newton sounded irritated.

He strode across to grab hold of Norman and find out whether he had actually got as far as speaking to either of the carriage drivers. While he remonstrated with the boy, Abigail walked on.

A crowd gathered further down the quay; attracted by the sound of laughter, Abigail hurried. Standing on tiptoe and still unable to see, she pushed through. From the sarcastic oohs and aahs, it was clear the onlookers were enjoying the spectacle of an argument; she could hear raised voices, but couldn't catch what they were saying.

When Abigail had elbowed her way to the front, she stood on the edge of the quay opposite the broken-masted ketch. Snarled rigging was strewn over the deck and a rust-coloured sail was tangled amongst it. In the centre of the deck a stump of splintered white wood jutted up where the mainmast should have been — held by the rigging, the broken mast and its spars floated helpless, now parallel with the hull.

In the middle of this chaos of rope and canvas, a police constable held a young woman, hardly more than a girl, by her arms. Wearing a dirty shift dress, the girl was as thin as wire. She had bronzed skin, a narrow face and her hair was just a tangle of black. She screamed at him, spat, and tried to twist herself free. The constable's hat rolled on to the deck at their feet. A good head and shoulders taller than her and with broad, strong shoulders, he held her like a doll. As the girl struggled to lash out with her fists and yelled curses in his face, he turned for approval to the jeering crowd; his mouth sloped in a lopsided grin. The more the crowd catcalled, the more the woman fought. She tried to wrench her arms free, hacked at his shins with her bare feet, shoved at him and pulled away — nothing worked. The crowd loved it. They all knew the constable and called him by name. They yelled suggestions as to what he should do with this wildcat and jokingly suggested prize money for the winner; some of the men even offered to lend him a hand.

But the constable was stuck; the woman refused to give up. The crowd watched the realization dawn in his grinning face that sooner or later he was going to have to let her go. And what was going to happen then? The crowd knew this too; they egged him on.

The woman sensed his confusion; she drew back her head and looked him in the eye. The grin was still slapped across his face; he was enjoying holding her like a trophy in front of everyone. He wasn't going to let her go. She jerked her head forward and caught him on the bridge of the nose. Blood exploded over his face. As he yelped in pain, his instinct was to ratchet his grip tighter. He heard the crowd roar. He didn't know what to do. The pain drove a nail between his eyes. His head was full of noise. The woman continued to stare; she seemed to be daring him. Suddenly, he was afraid that she was going to do it again. He had no option; he lifted her bodily off the deck, held her for a moment, turned and pitched her over the side.

Instead of the roar of approval the constable expected, the crowd hushed as though the breath had been knocked out of each of them. A woman's voice shouted something; a rumble of conversation began about the girl's chances in the tide. The constable stared helplessly into their faces. A second ago they had been cheering; now they blamed him. He turned to the river. The girl was already being taken midstream, yards from the side of the boat; her dark hair just visible against the churning water. As he watched, she was towed under. In the crowd, all sound died.

Then there was someone on the deck with him. A woman in a feathered hat was pulling at the buttons of her jacket. She was shouting something at him, but he couldn't tell what it was; her accent sounded so strange. He couldn't tell whether she wanted him to do something or get out of the way so he just stood there and let her barge past him. The woman flung away her jacket, leaned down and pulled at her boots. All he could think was that the boots were scarlet and he had never seen boots that colour before.

In the crowd, shouts crackled like gunfire. As the constable watched, the woman kicked her boots across the deck, stumbled over the torn rigging, stepped up on to the gunwale and, still with the peacock feather dancing above her hat, jumped.

# 2

*One week earlier*

'I want your complete assurance that Newton is your best man, Chief Inspector.' Sir Lawrence Yare MP frowned; he seemed to be making up his mind about something.

In his hand he held a single vellum sheet, a hand-delivered letter, which he had just finished reading. He stood with his back to the grate and gestured Chief Inspector Gillis to join him; the coal fire had not yet taken the chill out of the air.

A private room on the first floor of the Samson Club had been reserved in Sir Lawrence's name for this meeting. Between the leather armchairs pulled up in front of the fireplace was a low table on which lay a short-barrelled pistol and a box of cartridges. Mid-morning light filtered in through the high window which overlooked St James's.

'I require an officer of the highest calibre to escort and guard a member of the Canadian parliament, who is currently a guest of Her Majesty's government. A vessel containing a shipment of Fenian weapons has been blown ashore on the Devonshire coast. I want the visitor to inspect them.'

Sir Lawrence wore a black wool frockcoat with a satin collar; a diamond pin held his necktie in place. His thin face was dominated by an eagle nose and pale eyes, the same features which could be seen in the portraits of his ancestors, stretching back to Cromwell's time, which lined the hallways of his family seat. Tall and narrow-shouldered, he had a tendency to lean towards people as he talked as if he was a crow about to peck them; having been called to the Bar in his youth, he was accustomed to eliciting the information he wanted.

'Inspector Newton is a fine officer.' Gillis did not hesitate. 'His abilities would be particularly suited to this assignment.'

Gillis was short and square-shouldered. His hair was oiled and precisely parted; his side whiskers and neat moustache were combed. A starched collar cut uncomfortably into the flesh of his neck. He spoke in clipped phrases, suitable for giving straight answers to straight questions.

'Newton's father used to be a member here, although I never knew him.' Sir Lawrence was fishing. 'There was talk of bankruptcy.'

'Newton distinguished himself on the

North West Frontier . . . ' Gillis countered.

'I heard he resigned his commission, trouble paying his mess bills.'

'I wouldn't know about that, Sir Lawrence.' Gillis briefly inspected the rug beneath his feet.

Sir Lawrence pursed his lips; he knew more than Gillis did.

'Invested in a Manchester cotton mill,' Sir Lawrence elaborated. 'When the American war broke out, cotton imports dried up overnight. No cotton, no mill. Investors lost the lot.'

'I understand Inspector Newton was not in favour of his father's financial dealings.' Something told Gillis he was saying too much.

Sir Lawrence let the silence weigh heavily on the atmosphere of the room.

'On account of the slavery issue,' Gillis felt he had to explain. 'The cotton being produced on plantations.'

'An idealist.' Sir Lawrence smiled; he had won a piece of information. He quickly put two and two together. 'So after a row, he went off to fight for queen and country and when he came home, the family silver was no more.'

'He distinguished himself in the Hyde Park riots.' Gillis tried to steer the focus of the discussion. 'Kept a clear head, rallied the constables. His decisive actions ensured the safety of a great number.'

'This assignment is hardly comparable with a Reform League riot, Chief Inspector.' The sarcasm was deliberate. Sir Lawrence continued to probe.

'Inspector Newton is an educated man.' Gillis refused to give up. 'His family background . . . '

'Not just a man of action, but someone able to hold his own in society.' Sir Lawrence plucked the meaning from behind Gillis's words. He smiled again; he had what he needed.

Just as he finished speaking, there was a knock at the door; a porter announced Inspector Theodore Newton.

'You come with a high recommendation from the chief inspector, Newton.'

Sir Lawrence did not bother to introduce himself. Without moving from the fire he beckoned Newton to approach. He matched the man he saw in front of him against the information he had previously been given. He leaned forward.

'I hope you can live up to it.'

Arriving precisely on time, Newton strode confidently across the room. He greeted Sir Lawrence and the chief inspector with professional courtesy. He appeared indifferent to the luxurious decoration of the room, the panelled walls, carved mantelpiece and ancient faded kilim on which Sir Lawrence and Gillis stood; his eyes fixed on the gun on the table.

Sir Lawrence gestured the other men to sit while he himself continued to stand with his back to the fire. He held up the letter.

'This need not change our plan,' he said. 'I invited Mr March, a member of the new Canadian parliament, to join us this morning. Made millions exporting timber to Europe apparently. I had intended to ask you to escort him to Devonshire. This letter informs me that he was struck down by bronchitis on the voyage and is confined to his bed. In a few minutes, his daughter will join us as his representative.'

'Daughter?' Gillis stared.

Sir Lawrence held up his hand for silence.

'There have been Fenian attacks in Canada and bomb plots here. It is imperative for the security of both countries that we forge links with the Dominion police. We must be able to share intelligence concerning all suspected individuals, dynamiters and terrorists, whoever and wherever they are.'

Sir Lawrence's mouth drew tight. He stared briefly out of the window.

'Some of my parliamentary colleagues maintain that the Fenian threat to our shores is on the wane. They are fond of saying that the Clerkenwell bomb was five years ago and we need no longer fear attack. Last week, the discovery of a shipment of arms on the Devonshire coast proved them wrong.'

Newton listened intently. He had witnessed the carnage in Clerkenwell himself: twelve dead, over a hundred injured. He was unaware that more weapons had been discovered.

'As a Member of Parliament, I proposed to establish and lead a Special Advisory Board with ties to the Home Office and Scotland Yard more than twelve months ago.' Sir Lawrence leaned forward again. 'Time and again, this proposal has been blocked. Factions within the government wish to play down the Fenian threat; they do not realize that just because present policy towards Ireland advocates Home Rule, it does not obviate the danger. They dismiss all discussion as alarmist.'

Sir Lawrence had rehearsed his evidence; he looked accusingly at each of them.

'Last year there was another attempt on the life of Her Majesty. A Fenian attempt.'

'Arthur O'Connor had no ball in his pistol.' Gillis pulled himself upright; this was too much. 'He was not a Fenian. He was a

17-year-old boy who was not right in his mind.'

'He claimed to be a Fenian,' Sir Lawrence snapped. 'What is the difference between a man with a gun who claims to be a Fenian and a man with a gun who *is* a Fenian?'

He shifted from foot to foot with irritation.

'May I also remind you that it was the Queen's ghillie who came between Her Majesty and her assailant, not an officer of the Metropolitan Police?'

He paused to let them consider the implication.

'You both saw the damage at Clerkenwell,' Sir Lawrence continued. 'Did the Metropolitan Police fail to heed the warning they received before this outrage?'

Gillis stared at the floor.

'I rest my case.' Already pale, further colour drained from Sir Lawrence's thin cheeks. 'I am ideally suited to leading a Special Advisory Board and such a position merits a seat in Cabinet.'

He paused and stared into their faces, trying to decide if he needed to provide further explanation.

'In my father's time, men from Irish estates came willingly as navigators to this country to build the canals and to help the country prosper; now they leave on boats for America and, once they get there, fall under Fenian malevolence. Loyal subjects are turned into enemies of Her Majesty. An iron fist is required. The malign influence is worldwide, the United States, Canada, Australia, this country, even France. By inviting Mr March to these shores, I intend to establish a close relationship with the Dominion, between their new police force and our own Scotland Yard. I am determined.'

He crumpled the sheet of notepaper in his fist and flung it into the fire.

'I shall certainly not be thwarted by bronchitis or any other damn ailment.' He glared at the two men. 'Therefore we shall proceed with Miss March.'

'Sir Lawrence . . . ' Gillis protested.

Sir Lawrence gestured him to be quiet.

'She acts as her father's amanuensis. According to his testimonial she is intelligent and knowledgeable. Anyway, we have no choice.' Sir Lawrence paused. 'I understand she even followed a course of medical studies. Although, naturally she was not able to sit the examinations, being a woman.'

'If we take her to Clerkenwell . . . ' Gillis said.

'We shall not let her anywhere near Clerkenwell,' Sir Lawrence thundered. Gillis's interruptions exasperated him. 'Even now, repairs are not completed. The scale of the dynamiting will make us look ridiculous. And, might I add, make the investigators of the Metropolitan Police look particularly ridiculous.'

He stared out of the window at the breadth of the sky.

'Our purpose is to inspire confidence; we must show that we are successful in combating this threat.' Sir Lawrence was resolute. 'We shall allow Miss March to view the haul of arms in Devonshire, proof that even in the far corners of the realm our Borough Police are alert to Fenian danger.' He turned to Newton. 'You will accompany her. You will make sure she appreciates how severe the threat is and how effective we are at countering it. Then you will oversee the freighting of the weapons back to London.' Sir Lawrence stared out of the window again. 'Having seen the weapons at first hand, Miss March will pass a cogent message to her father which he will transmit, in due course, to the Dominion parliament: they will appreciate the pressing need for us to stand together and under my direction, we shall be successful in thwarting the Fenian scoundrels.'

Sir Lawrence examined the faces of the two men; he wanted to be sure they had understood.

'If I am to act as bodyguard, I request that I be armed,' Newton said.

Sir Lawrence pointed to the gun on the table.

'The Webley .450, better known as the British Bulldog.' There was a note of pride in his voice. 'A new five-shot repeating pistol. Next year these will come into commission. You will be the first metropolitan officer to carry one, Inspector.' Then he added, 'I have arranged for a young sergeant from the Irish police to accompany you, a most loyal and trustworthy man. He has carried out undercover work against Fenian cells in the past. He travels down by train from Liverpool today.'

'Irish?' Gillis said.

Sir Lawrence glared.

Newton picked up the gun and checked the chamber. The wooden grip sat comfortably in his hand. He felt the weight of it, held it up to examine the snub barrel and the double action. Aware that Sir Lawrence was still speaking, he slipped it into his jacket pocket and picked up the box of shells.

'When you return from Devonshire, I shall write to the Home Secretary and inform him that the threat is still great, it is current and that I am successfully dealing with it: this haul of weapons will be the proof. The local

Borough Police have secured the guns; the vessel which transported them is under guard.'

'This Irish sergeant . . . ' Gillis would not be put off.

'My task is to persuade the Home Secretary,' Sir Lawrence sighed with irritation. 'Yours, Chief Inspector, is to oversee the work of Inspector Newton and Sergeant Culley and to report to me. I have instructed Culley to call at Scotland Yard as soon as he arrives in London.' Sir Lawrence paused; he leaned over Gillis. 'I need hardly spell out to you that if this is mishandled, the consequences will be severe.'

Before Gillis could ask anything else, there was a knock at the door. The servant who showed Newton up entered and handed Sir Lawrence a note.

'Yes, yes.'

He waved dismissively.

'Miss March has arrived,' Sir Lawrence announced. 'This being a gentleman's club, she will be shown up by the back stairs.'

The interruption caused Sir Lawrence to lose his flow. He turned to Newton.

'Your father was a member here, I understand.'

'He was.' Newton's face reddened; he avoided Sir Lawrence's penetrating stare.

'You decided not to follow in his footsteps.'

'That's correct.' Newton refused to be drawn.

After another quiet knock at the door, an assistant porter showed a young woman into the room. Gillis and Newton jumped to their feet.

Abigail wore a fashionable jacket, skirt and gloves; a luxurious peacock feather swayed over her hat. But as soon as she entered, the eyes of all three men fell to her feet. The toes of red silk boots peeped out from under her skirt.

'Sir Lawrence.' Smiling warmly, she stepped towards him with her hand outstretched. 'Gentlemen.'

It was just as her father had warned her: the back stairs, the uneasy glances, the men standing like sentries, Sir Lawrence's cursory enquiries as to her father's health.

Abigail had met too many politicians to be taken in by Sir Lawrence's charm, but his detailed knowledge impressed her. He demonstrated how the British North America Act established the Dominion and gave a thorough account of how the Fenian attack on Campobello was repulsed by ships from Halifax. He was adamant that cooperation between the British government and the new Canadian parliament was the way to make the civilized world safe; he emphasized the role he was suited to play in this. If he was concerned about her sex, he did not show it. He had bigger fish to fry.

The two policemen were a different matter. Chief Inspector Gillis was surly and suspicious. At first, she thought this was merely the usual prejudice. But as Sir Lawrence continued to speak, she noticed Gillis awkwardly run a finger round the inside of his collar. He looked thunderous. If he had been a schoolboy, you would have said he was bored, but since he was a chief inspector with the Metropolitan Police in the presence of a Member of Parliament, she guessed he was being overruled.

Inspector Newton was different again. Made even more apprehensive by the presence of a woman than the chief inspector (she smiled at how Newton blushed when she shook his hand and looked aside when she caught his eye), his lower rank meant he was unconcerned with political manoeuvring. It allowed him a naturalness which the two others lacked. His stiff stance in the presence of his superiors suggested that being here was a trial for him too. She warmed to him.

'This is a war of shadows,' Sir Lawrence proclaimed. 'Her Majesty herself is in danger.' He glared at Gillis. 'Let us not forget

Prince Alfred was shot and wounded in Australia. The colonials set an example to us all; they strung the Fenian wretch from the gibbet within the month.'

'With respect sir, the Prince tried to intervene on the man's behalf.' Gillis tried again. 'He was never proved to be under orders from the Fenian Brotherhood as he claimed.'

'Exactly my point, Chief Inspector.' Sir Lawrence rounded on him. 'These individuals claim to be acting for the Fenians because they believe they are. If a fellow has a pistol in his hand and points it at a member of our Royal Family believing he is acting on behalf of the Fenian Brotherhood, then he might as well be.'

Sir Lawrence looked from one to the other of them to make sure they followed. He lowered his voice.

'Who is to say the Fenian Brotherhood will not send their dynamiters to Buckingham Palace? There have been five attempts on the life of Her Majesty. Who is to say there will not be more? The latest man to wave a gun was an Irishman.'

'There was no ball in it.' Gillis looked sour. 'The man was a lunatic. The others were equally unbalanced.'

Colour rose above Sir Lawrence's stiff

collar. He sniffed sharply; the line of his mouth was cruel.

'I agree with Sir Lawrence.' Abigail's sing-song confidence took the men by surprise. They stared.

'We had an assassination in Canada five years ago. One of our members of the new parliament, Mr McGee, who was known for his stance against the Fenian Brotherhood, was shot after a late sitting. The assassins waited for him outside his home.'

Silence fell like a guillotine; the men were lost for words. Sir Lawrence had not anticipated validation from a female from the Dominion; Gillis choked because a woman seemed to have flat-out contradicted him; Newton was silenced because Abigail's forthrightness so obviously disconcerted his superiors.

'And I agree with you, Chief Inspector.' Abigail smiled at Gillis. 'This is a matter which could easily become exaggerated in the newspapers; it is vital to avoid public panic.'

'Well, I must say ... ' An embarrassed smile touched the corners of Sir Lawrence's mouth. He hurried to pursue the subject. 'A boat containing a haul of rifles has been wrecked on the Devon coast. I wish you to inspect the weapons before they are trans-ported to London. I wish you to see at first hand the threat that we face and that even as far away as northern Devonshire, our Borough Police are alert to the danger. Inspector Newton and a sergeant will accompany you, Miss March, provided your father is in agreement.'

Abigail felt Newton look at her; when she caught his eye, his gaze fell away.

'There is no danger,' Sir Lawrence added quickly. 'The captain and the crew are scattered.'

'Do we know the size of the shipment?' Gillis asked.

'The local Borough Police have all the details.' A shadow of annoyance crossed Sir Lawrence's face. 'They are the ones who hold the wreck under guard.'

'Contraband of that sort tends to go missing,' Gillis said.

Sir Lawrence ignored him.

That afternoon, Newton arranged for train tickets to be purchased and a telegram sent to Superintendent Rawle of the Bideford Borough Police which informed him of their imminent arrival and requested him to arrange accommodation for two men and a woman at a local hotel.

# 3

The second the two women started to spew river water, the crowd went wild. People elbowed for a view from the quay or craned over the bridge parapet to stare at the two half-drowned bodies retching out their guts on the deck of the fishing boat: they had witnessed a miracle. A woman had snatched another human being from the flood tide and saved her life. The story ran through the crowd that the second woman had been thrown in the river by a constable and the first had launched herself in to save her. 'Which constable?' people asked. When they heard Lamb's name, they fell silent.

On the quay, the crowd shifted aside. Lizzie Hookway sent men over from the Newfoundland Inn with an old door to act as a stretcher. Newton directed them to take Abigail first, but she waved them away and pointed to the girl. Clutching the blanket with bony hands, the girl's arms were thin; the shape of her skull was visible through her skin; she lay shivering with blue lids closed over her eyes.

A carriage drew up on the quay. A young

man climbed out, someone else nobody knew. Demanding to know what was going on in an Irish accent, he shoved through, called out Newton's name and looked as though he was about to jump down on to the deck where Newton stood over the women. Newton turned, shouted something and pointed back down the quay.

Reddened by the river water, Abigail's eyes were open. She pulled the blanket round her and propped herself up on one elbow; a coughing fit racked her chest. Her face was milky grey, her lips white; her dark hair straggled in knots over her shoulders. The thin blanket did nothing to stop her shaking.

'We must get you in front of a fire.' Newton did his best to sound cheerful.

Seeing Abigail like this was like standing on a beach and feeling a receding wave pull the sand away under his feet. He struggled to help her up. His admiration was palpable; he deferred to her over everything. Wouldn't she rather wait for the men to return with the door? Did she think it wise to attempt to walk? At the same time, he wanted to protect her; sympathy wrenched at him as he looked at her white face and pale determined mouth and watched her shudder with cold beneath the blanket. Gently, he helped her to her feet and waved a path through the crowd.

The air in the parlour bar of the Newfoundland Inn was a comforting fug of woodsmoke, tobacco and apples. Faggots made of briar and ivy crackled in the grate. Lizzie Hookway brought more blankets and dry clothes down the narrow stairs and pushed a pair of high-backed carver chairs close to the hearth. She announced that the bar was closed, bellowed at the men to get out, drew the cotton curtains across the bays and locked the door. Finding himself swept unceremoniously out on to the quay along with the drinkers, Newton headed off in search of his boots.

The *Brianna* was a two-masted ketch, fore and aft rigged. The mizzen was still in place, but the mainmast had been snapped off five feet above the deck; it lay alongside in the water, still joined to the vessel by a tangle of rigging and sailcloth. Constable Lamb sat on the deck, leaned his head back against the stump of the mast and cradled his face in his hands.

'This is the boat, sir,' Culley called to him. 'The constable here claims the woman was in the hold and sprang out at him, followed him out on deck apparently. He says he was obliged to grab hold of her to stop her attacking him.'

Culley pointed at Lamb's bloody face.

'Telling me you didn't lay a hand on her?'

Culley leaned over the constable and glared at him. The constable cupped his hands over his swollen nose.

'I had to keep hold of her,' he moaned. 'She had a knife in her belt.'

'She was a girl,' Culley sneered. 'You telling me you never shoved her over the side?'

Newton let Culley continue with his questions while he scanned the deck in search of his boots.

'What were you doing down in the hold anyway?'

Lamb whimpered under the onslaught.

'You sure you didn't drag her down there?'

Lamb took his hands away from his face. His nose was purple like a fruit; there was blood in his teeth.

'What are you asking me all this for? What do you mean you're from the Metropolitan?'

'The hold.' Newton pulled on his boots. 'Anything down there?'

'Empty, sir.' Lamb tried to sit up straight. His fingers went back to cradling his nose. 'I went down there to have a look around; the woman had hidden herself in the bows. I was supposed to stay on deck and run to the station if any of the crew turned up.'

'You're telling me she sailed in on the boat and no one found her?' Newton glared at him. 'She can recognize the crew; she prob-ably witnessed where the guns were loaded.'

'I can't say, sir.' Lamb was crestfallen. 'All I know is — '

'The crew?' Newton said. 'What about them?'

'Ran off when she went aground. No one's seen 'em.'

Lamb traced the contours of his swollen nose with the tips of his fingers.

'When?'

'A few days ago. A farmer reported the vessel washed up on the skern.'

Apart from a group of men waiting outside the Newfoundland Inn, the crowd had dispersed. Shoppers made their way back up the High Street; pedestrians moved across the bridge; children went back to their games amongst the mooring ropes. The river flowed fast, churning over its sandy bed, bearing gifts of broken branches and blackened driftwood which snagged under the arches of the bridge.

'What's happened to her? The girl who . . . ' Lamb plucked up courage; his voice shook. 'She ain't drowned, is she?'

'No thanks to you,' Newton said. 'Mrs Hookway is caring for her.'

'Lizzie will make sure she's all right.' Lamb sounded relieved. 'I never meant . . . '

'Never mind what you never meant,' Culley snapped.

Newton retrieved the jacket he'd flung across the deck, shook it and pulled it on.

'Continue your questioning, Sergeant. You can report back to me later. I shall call at the Newfoundland Inn and then make my way to the police station.'

Newton pushed through the crowd which had gathered outside the Newfoundland Inn, pounded on the door and called out. His heart crashed in his chest; suddenly his desire to see Abigail overrode everything. The thought of her lying in distress made him feel hollowed out. Eventually, the door opened a few inches; Lizzie Hookway's face glared.

'I ain't letting no one in,' she said fiercely. 'Especially no gentlemen.'

Newton jammed his foot in the door.

'There's nothing to worry your head about; both the ladies are recovered and resting by the fire.' Lizzie Hookway forced herself to be polite. 'I shall endeavour to get them to take a little broth later. Come back this evening if you wish to see how things are.'

'Miss March is under my protection and I wish to speak to her now.'

Lizzie Hookway was used to barring men who wanted to come in through this door.

'I've told you,' she warned.

Newton heard her drag a chain across. He drove his shoulder against the door, but the chain held.

'Mrs Hookway.' He bit his tongue. 'I am grateful for the trouble you have taken but I repeat Miss March's father has entrusted me with her protection . . . '

'In that case, you ain't done too good a job of it, have you?'

'Mrs Hookway, I am an officer of the Metropolitan Police.'

'I don't care if you're the Shah of Persia, these ladies are in no fit state to be talked to by you or anybody else.'

Abigail appeared at Lizzie Hookway's shoulder. Still pale, her face had regained a little of its natural colour; her damp hair hung in twists over her shoulders. She held a blanket tightly around her. She tried to speak but her voice was almost lost.

'Miss March.' Relief choked Newton. 'I'm glad to see . . . '

Lizzie Hookway ushered Abigail away from the door.

'Miss March . . . ' Newton called after her.

His foot still wedged the door; he watched Lizzie Hookway place her arm round Abigail's shoulder and escort her to the fireside where a wooden chair was lined with blankets. After she tucked more blankets over the young woman's knees, she returned to the door.

'She was sleeping,' Lizzie Hookway hissed. 'And you've woke her.'

'The other,' Newton said. 'The woman from the boat, is she . . . '

Lizzie Hookway launched a powerful kick which dislodged Newton's foot, slammed the door and rattled the bolt across.

An old man who sat on the bench below the window cradled the bowl of his clay pipe and looked up at Newton.

'Don't do no good to upset Lizzie.'

Newton pretended he hadn't heard. He looked round for someone to ask directions to the police station, but the few onlookers who'd witnessed the confrontation drifted away. Newton was forced to turn back to the old man.

\* \* \*

When the Borough Police Force was created, a suite of high-ceilinged rooms on the first floor of the town hall building was designated headquarters. Superintendent Oliver Rawle was a short, wiry, thin-faced man with clipped whiskers and dark hair oiled straight back from his forehead. His desk was a model of order; precisely piled papers were arranged beside an open ledger, a glass inkwell, a collection of steel-nibbed pens, sealing wax and a blotter. A pen was in his hand and a blank sheet in front of him. When Newton knocked and entered without waiting for a reply, Rawle sprang to his feet.

'Expecting you,' he said quickly. 'Just applying my mind to a memorandum of matters for discussion.'

Newton dispensed with the introductions. He had no inclination to make small talk and the last thing he wanted was to undergo interrogation about the events on the quay.

'This boat that you had towed: I understand that the crew ran off. Have you apprehended any of them? What about the skipper?'

Rawle was a stickler for efficiency; he prided himself on his meticulous record keeping. He insisted all his constables note down contemporaneous accounts of every arrest, charge and run-in with local miscreants. Not only was he able to place these notes at a moment's notice in the hands of anyone who asked, he knew for a fact that neighbouring forces did no such thing. Now, this inspector from Scotland Yard barged in and fired a fusillade of questions which implied that he was slipshod in his duties. His resentment simmered.

'Have you apprehended anyone?' Newton repeated.

'We have not,' Rawle said. 'I can only assume that the crew made their escape when the boat ran aground or else they were lost at sea.'

Typical Scotland Yard, Rawle thought: ambitious and patronizing. He had never met a policeman from the capital who had the first idea of what it took to run a borough force. In London they had an army of constables; he had a handful. Low pay and the insistence on literacy made recruitment a nightmare. This Inspector Newton had the whole of the Metropolitan force behind him; down here Rawle personally carried the can.

'What about the rifles?'

'Accounted for and safe.' Rawle smiled. He had the answer ready; no one could fault him on efficiency. 'Five cases are under lock and key downstairs in one of the cells.'

'I wish to see them,' Newton said.

As if I haven't got anything better to do, Rawle thought. Why couldn't Newton simply take his word for it? He got to his feet and gestured towards the door.

'I understood a representative of the Canadian parliament was to inspect the weapons.'

Newton outlined what had happened on the quay.

'We are most fortunate Miss March is a strong swimmer. A life was saved.'

'You are suggesting that a woman was pitched into the Torridge by one of my constables?' Rawle was stunned. He halted halfway down the stairs.

'Constable Lamb,' Newton said.

For a moment, Rawle was speechless. Who did Newton think he was?

'Preposterous. I cannot believe . . . ' He caught Newton's eye. 'I shall speak to the constable personally; I shall insist on a full report.'

The cellar had been converted into two narrow stone cells. Light was thin; the walls ran with moisture. Below ground, this close to the river the temperature dropped by many degrees. In one of the cells, five matchwood crates were lined up. The lids had been jemmied and replaced, but not nailed. Wisps of straw from the packing littered the floor.

Newton pulled off the nearest lid. Six Enfield rifle-muskets were lined up nose to tail. Newton picked one up and held it up to the light from the barred window. The stock and barrel were flaked with dry mud, the flip-up sight was skewed and the trigger was stiff with rust. He replaced it and picked up a second gun. Rawle couldn't wait for Newton to leave; having to stand there and watch him peer at useless old firearms was excruciating. He had to find out what happened on the quay from one of his own men.

'They're all in this condition,' Rawle said, trying to put a patch on things. 'If Scotland Yard will foot the bill, I could arrange for a gunsmith to restore them.'

'Transport them to London as they are,' Newton said brusquely; he wanted to leave no doubt as to who was in charge.

As soon as he left the police station, Newton went straight to his hotel. Culley's signature was in the register, but the hall porter told him that the sergeant had left his key and gone out; he had seen him talking to one of the local constables outside the hotel entrance.

Newton hurried along to the Newfoundland Inn. He was determined to be the first to know when the girl was in a fit state to answer questions. He was surprised by the sense of anticipation which rose in him, knowing that he would also see Abigail. At that moment, his concern for her welfare was paramount. He had not begun to think how he would explain the fact that she had thrown herself into the river whilst under his charge.

To Newton's surprise, the inn was open for business. The smell of sour cider and the wreaths of blue tobacco smoke which lay in the air made him catch his breath. As he stepped inside, the drinkers looked up and the rumble of conversation hushed. Lizzie Hookway, bearing a tray laden with pint pots, pushed through the crowd.

'She's awake.' She glowered resentfully at Newton. 'Wait here and I'll ask if she wishes to see you.'

A few moments later, she beckoned from the top of the stairs.

In the modest bedroom, the air was warmed by a coal fire. Pale evening light filled the room from the bay window which overlooked the quay. Huddled up to the neck under blankets, Abigail lay propped against a bank of pillows. Some colour had returned to her cheeks; her silky hair was brushed over her shoulders. She smiled when Newton pushed open the door.

'Lizzie made such a fuss of us.' Abigail's voice was hardly more than a whisper. 'She makes the most excellent nurse. I told her that one day when I am allowed to work in a hospital, she must come and help me on the wards.'

Newton wanted to laugh out loud when he saw how complete Abigail's recovery was. Then he remembered.

'The girl . . . '

'Catalin. She is recovered like I am and was

lying here with me.'

'You spoke to her?' Newton leaned forward to catch what Abigail was saying.

'Lizzie made us the most nourishing broth and . . . '

'Catalin? Where is she now?'

Newton's detective's instincts jolted. This was not right. The girl had almost drowned; she should be here still.

'I fell asleep. When I woke she had gone.'

'Did you find out . . . ?'

'She said as soon as she recovered her strength she wanted to get back to the boat.' Abigail's voice began to disappear.

Newton had the sensation of sand slipping through his fingers.

'Abigail, I came to question her. She is a witness. I must . . . '

'She speaks a little French.'

As a dry cough seized her throat, Abigail reached for the glass beside the bed; she waved for him to go.

Vinegar-coloured clouds towered above the town but the sky was not yet dark. The tide had receded so far that the boats rested on river mud. Newton ran the length of the quay.

The *Brianna* lay half on her side. The piles of rigging and sailcloth slid to the far edge of the deck; her broken mast lay beside the hull on the mud. Newton called out Catalin's name, but there was no answer. He called out for Constable Lamb. No answer. The drop from the quayside to the deck was six feet. He scrambled over the edge and lowered himself. The deck was wet and sloped at forty-five degrees; his feet slid away under him.

Newton worked his way along to the hatches on his hands and knees. One of the coverings was unbolted and thrown open. The hold was pitch dark and smelled of chaff; when he called out, his voice echoed. He had to be sure. There was a stepladder propped against the edge of the hatch. He called out again.

'I am Inspector Newton of the Metropolitan Police. There is no need to be afraid. I am Miss March's friend. I mean you no harm.'

He stepped over the side of the hatch on to the rungs of the ladder.

'Catalin. I am Abigail's friend.'

Below the level of the deck, the hold was airless. Dust dried his throat; the smell of hessian sacks choked him. At the bottom of the ladder, he took a step into the darkness. Certain this was where the girl was hiding, he called out again. Then his foot caught against something. This wasn't right. The hold was empty so why were there sacks left behind? He reached down. It took a split second for him to realize that far from being some abandoned piece of cargo, his hand was touching a girl's face.

Newton stood up sharply. The darkness pressed on his temples; the square of half-light from the hatch overhead offered no relief. His first instinct was to scramble back up the ladder to where he could breathe. His heart crashed in his chest. He forced himself to stand still, made himself be calm. He heard himself repeat the girl's name, softly this time, as if he were talking to her. He reached down again.

The body was as light as a child's and still warm. Newton laid it over his shoulder, the arms hanging loosely behind him. He gripped the sides of the ladder and pulled himself up, rung by rung. The girl must have slipped on the deck and fallen; maybe she had been hurrying so as not to be seen. As she held back the hatch, she must have missed her footing on the ladder.

Newton lifted the girl's body off his shoulders out on to the sloping deck. In the grey evening light, he saw that she was wearing a woollen coat over a long nightdress. Her eyes were closed and her hair was brushed. But he was wrong about the fall. There was a wide gash across the front of her neck where someone had cut her throat.

# 4

Newton hauled himself out onto the deck. All the air was knocked out of him as if he was winded. He felt sick; his thoughts spun. He couldn't look at the body. The girl was so frail. She smelled of lavender soap; Lizzie Hookway must have washed her hair. The tear across her throat was savage. He imagined the force it must have taken to make it; the blade must have been blunt with rust. His boots skidded on the wet wood as he reached for the side of the boat. He couldn't stand, let alone haul himself up on to the quay from here. Clinging to the gunwale, he raised his head and searched the line of vessels for a light.

Above him at the far end of the quay, there were voices; gusts of laughter echoed each time someone opened the door to the Newfoundland Inn, but they were too far away to hear him if he called. The evening faded fast; angry clouds built a fortress overhead and the wind cut through his jacket. Gulls screamed as they made their last flight of the day.

Calmer now, Newton allowed himself to

glance back. The girl lay against the hatch, her head resting on a pile of rigging. She looked innocent and young as if she had made herself comfortable there and fallen asleep. In the remains of daylight, the gash across her neck was barely visible.

Newton pulled himself upright. Standing on the gunwale, he hauled himself along the mooring line until he could see over the edge of the quay. A hundred yards away, candles lit the windows of the Newfoundland Inn. All the doors were shut along the row of houses facing the river, the shop windows were dark and there were lights in the upstairs rooms. The carriages which had stood by the slip-ways had gone and the cobbles were empty. He made a massive effort, heaved himself up from the gunwale on to the quay and took a last look down at the girl. Darkness covered her body like a quilt.

Where the hell was Culley? The thought burst in Newton's head. Hadn't he instructed him to find the search party? Didn't that mean going from boat to boat on the quay? The sea wind slashed through his clothes and rattled the teeth in his head. Then he reminded himself he sent Culley off to hunt for information because he wanted to call at the Newfoundland Inn and check on Abigail; he didn't want his sergeant trailing after him with his cynical grin.

Newton clutched his arms round himself and ran. He steered clear of the light from the inn windows and turned up Bridge Street. In his office, Rawle was tidying his desk ready to go home. When Newton burst in he threw back his chair and jumped to his feet.

'Good God ... ' Rawle's voice trailed away.

'Where are the night watch?' Newton thundered. 'There's the body of a murdered girl on the *Brianna*.'

'Look at the state of you, you look as if you've ... ' It took Rawle a second to comprehend what Newton was saying. 'Get yourself next to the fire.'

'The girl,' Newton bellowed.

'I heard you. What girl?' Rawle was at a loss. 'What are you saying?'

'The girl who was on the boat, the one whom your constable threw into the river, our only witness.'

The door burst open. The sergeant Newton had barged past at the front desk stood there, a question mark in his face.

'Sir?' He saw Rawle's expresson. 'Is everything — ?'

'Where are the watch?' Rawle rounded on him.

'On their routes, both of them.' The

sergeant looked as if he wished he'd stayed downstairs. 'They left an hour ago.'

'But where?' Exasperation strained Rawle's voice. 'At this moment?'

Newton stood in front of the fire while the two of them haggled over in which precise street the constables might be. Rawle dispatched the sergeant in search of the one they reckoned to be nearest the quay.

'Why is there no patrol on the quay?' Newton could not hide his contempt.

'Where is your sergeant?' Rawle would not take the blame. 'Why is he not helping us? You see how undermanned we are here.'

Standing close to the fire made steam rise from Newton's wet clothes; the heat was just as uncomfortable as the cold.

'The watch will be relieved at midnight by two other constables.' Rawle was defensive. He had no problems until Newton arrived; he was used to taking credit for the smooth operation of his station. 'I run an efficient station here, Inspector, even though I am short-handed. I have a whole town to see to.'

'There is a dead girl on one of the boats at the quayside,' Newton repeated.

'Then my sergeant will send for the undertaker,' Rawle exploded.

Newton refused to listen any more; he had no time for this pen pusher. He had to find

Culley. He stormed out of the office and down the stairs. Outside, he heard the blast of the sergeant's whistle sound a few streets away as he tried to contact the constable on watch. It was dark now. Black shadows made shapes in the spaces between the buildings; there was no moon. As the cold bit through his clothes, his thoughts raced.

Who would want the girl dead? This was no random killing, no furious stabbing by some drunken sailor. How could it be a robbery-gone-wrong? She had nothing to steal. Why had she left the fireside in Lizzie Hookway's upstairs room for the miserable emptiness of the *Brianna*? Whom had she gone to meet?

From the steps of the police station, Newton heard a second blast on the sergeant's whistle; a few streets away a shrill answer stabbed the night. A jolt of emotion which he did not recognize convulsed him. Fear? Surely not. The North West Frontier had cauterized him of fear; he believed he would never be afraid again. It was some anxiety he could not pin down; it had been with him since Abigail was pulled out of the river. He wanted to talk to her, to reassure himself that no harm had come to her. She was the last person to see the girl from the ketch alive.

The shriek of police whistles pierced the

darkness. A figure rounded the corner at the bottom of the street and hurried towards him.

'Sergeant?' Newton called. The word echoed.

Culley shouted something. When he got close, Newton smelled whiskey on his breath.

'I heard the whistles,' Culley said.

As Newton hurried them towards the Newfoundland Inn, he spilled out the news about the girl.

'Constable Lamb . . . ' Culley began.

'I'm not interested in that witless constable. Did you find out anything about the boat?'

Culley ran through what he had discovered. The *Brianna* had lost a mast and run aground on a salt marsh down the coast some time during the previous week. A local farmer rode into town to report the wreck. Only yesterday had the weather calmed enough for the vessel to be towed up the estuary. The skipper and crew had either scattered or drowned; no one knew.

'Anything about the rifles?' Newton cut Culley short.

'Five cases in the hold.'

Newton waited for more.

'The girl must have hidden herself well,' Culley said. 'They missed her when they searched.'

'I want a guard for Miss March.' Newton

quickened his pace. 'Day and night, until she recovers.'

'Best do that.' Culley was unsteady on his feet. 'She's a lovely girl.'

The overfamiliarity prickled; Newton stared at Culley but rather than be misinterpreted said nothing.

'Miss March says she will be out of bed in the morning as lying prostrate damages the constitution.' Culley was breathless keeping up with him. 'Mrs Hookway announced it in the bar.'

Conversation subsided as the two men opened the door to the Newfoundland Inn and elbowed through the drinkers. Newton headed for the stairs; he didn't stop to look for Lizzie Hookway. He knocked softly at the bedroom door. No answer. He turned the handle slowly and inched the door open. The bedside candle was extinguished and by the flickering firelight, Newton glimpsed Abigail asleep under a mound of bedclothes. Relief swept through him.

'Wait here.' He turned to Culley; his voice was a whisper. 'When I find a constable I shall send him to relieve you.'

'I found John Lamb earlier.' Culley caught Newton by the arm. 'I was on my way to tell you.'

'What about him?'

'He was downstairs in the bar foghorning about the girl he threw in the river.'

Culley's voice was low and urgent.

'He made everyone laugh describing what he should have done to her.'

'Was he drinking?'

'They teased him about his broken nose,' Culley said. 'It made him livid.'

'Was he drunk?'

'Not so much he didn't know what he was saying.'

'Where is he now?' Newton snapped.

'Home.' Culley looked at him. 'His shift is finished.'

'And what did he say he wanted to do to the girl?' Newton's expression was sour.

Culley drew him away from the bedroom door and dropped his voice to a whisper.

'He said he wished he'd slit her throat.'

'You heard this?'

'In front of witnesses,' Culley hissed.

★ ★ ★

The undertaker's handcart was parked alongside the *Brianna* when Newton reached the end of the quay. Quilliam, the undertaker, held up a lantern while a constable lifted the girl's body off the boat. Quilliam's sunken cheeks looked jaundiced in the lamplight; the corners of his mouth were turned down and satchels of skin hung under his eyes. He was pigeon-chested; Newton's first thought was that pushing the cart with a body on it would be too much for him, but as soon as the corpse was loaded, Quilliam pulled a sheet over it, nodded to the constable and took the cart by the handles. The big, wire-spoked wheels were oiled; the cart glided noiselessly along the quay towards the centre of town. Quilliam paced slowly behind it.

'Have you searched the boat?' Newton said.

The constable was busy retrieving his hat and lantern from the quayside. He moved slowly. The long jacket of his uniform was buttoned to the neck; handcuffs and a billy club hung from his belt. When he held up his lantern, Newton could see his face framed by heavy whiskers. He looked irritated.

'And who might you be?'

Before Newton could answer, the sergeant from the police station was at his elbow, lantern in hand. Out of breath from running, he was anxious to impress.

'Well? Have you searched as Inspector Newton asked?'

'No, Sergeant.' The man glanced nervously at Newton. 'The body was on the deck. Quilliam's took her.'

'Well, don't be standing about, get and search, then.'

As the constable lowered himself over the quayside, the sergeant passed down the lantern.

'Don't slip,' he warned. 'That deck don't look as if it's been scrubbed in a month.'

The lights in the upstairs windows of the houses along the quay were extinguished now; apart from the meagre glow from the bays of the Newfoundland Inn, the quay was dark. Wind picked up along the estuary; clouds hid the stars.

'Anything?' the sergeant called.

They could hear the constable moving about in the hold.

'South-westerly gales arrived the same time as spring tides.' The sergeant was anxious to fill a hole in the conversation. 'That's why so many vessels is moored; chased in on the storms last week, most of 'em. We got Welsh, Cornish, stone hackers from Caldy, you name it.'

'And this particular vessel,' Newton steered the conversation back to something relevant, 'broke her mast a week ago, is that right?'

The constable's head appeared through the hatch.

'Too dark, Sergeant. Can't see nothing. There ain't no one else down here, that's for sure. Neither dead nor alive.'

'Come on out, then,' the sergeant called. 'If there's more to find we'll find it in the morning.'

'Nothing at all?' Newton was not so easily satisfied.

'A blanket and a candle stowed far up in the bows.'

The constable climbed out of the hatch, handed up his lantern and reached for the sergeant to haul him up on to the quay.

Newton requested that the constable be allowed to stand guard outside Abigail's room in the Newfoundland Inn. Much to Newton's surprise, the sergeant agreed willingly. In fact, the sergeant seemed to have gone through a character change since he first met him earlier in the day. Now, nothing was too much trouble. Rawle's orders, Newton thought.

'Superintendent Rawle asked me to say he will see you in the morning at nine o'clock sharp,' the sergeant said. 'He has gone out to inspect the night watch on patrol. He then intends to view the body at the undertaker's chapel before he retires home for the evening. I shall return, lock up the station and then join him.'

Newton waved away the sergeant's offer of escorting him to his hotel and watched his lantern swing as he hurried away along the quay. Newton pulled his jacket round him and headed for the glow of yellow candlelight in the windows of the Newfoundland Inn. As mist rose from the river, the temperature fell. He listened to his own boot heels strike the cobbles, the creak of mooring ropes and the moan of the wind.

If Abigail was strong enough in the morning, Newton thought, they would inspect the cache of rifles in her presence and when she had seen enough to report back favourably to her father, they would head back to London. With the crew of the *Brianna* scattered and the only witness dead, an investigation into who smuggled the guns would take weeks and get nowhere. They would leave the girl's murder to Rawle and his men. Gillis would be satisfied; Sir Lawrence would be sent a copy of Abigail's report. Newton's primary concern was Abigail; Sir Lawrence would want her shepherded back to London. With luck, her dive into the river would become no more than a story for entertaining her friends at home.

# 5

First down for the hotel breakfast, Newton and Culley sat opposite each other across a table laid with a starched white cloth and heavy silver cutlery. Steam curled up from the twin spouts of a teapot and hot water jug; willow-pattern plates laden with eggs with golden yolks, thick slices of bacon and fat sausages sat in front of each them. Culley ploughed into his food without looking up.

'What possessed the girl?' Newton was at a loss. 'She went straight from a comfortable bed in the Newfoundland Inn to that filthy hold on the *Brianna*.'

'Meeting someone.' Culley waved a fork. 'She was probably with one of the crew, the skipper even.'

'On a ketch?' Newton shook his head.

'Eat up, sir.' Culley shovelled in another mouthful. 'This is good.'

'Did you see where the boat was from?'

'Duncormac.' Culley was determined to finish his breakfast. 'It's in County Wexford.'

'The girl wasn't Irish.' Newton sounded tentative. 'We know that much.'

'Could have been from anywhere.' Culley

shrugged. 'Hardly matters now.'

'She could have identified the smugglers.' Newton stabbed a forkful of bacon.

'She must have been half-daft,' Culley said. 'She knew the constables had taken the guns; it was a fair guess they would be watching the boat, but she headed straight back there.'

'Maybe one of the crew thought she'd given them up to the police. Came back to the boat to see if they could salvage anything, found her there and . . . ' Newton dug into his eggs.

'If the Borough Police had kept a proper watch on the vessel, this wouldn't have happened.' Culley looked round for a waiter to order more toast. 'Bet it shook you up finding her like that, eh, sir?'

'When I picked her up I couldn't believe how light she was.' Newton looked away. 'Skin and bone: the poor creature must have been half-starved.'

'Do you want me to ask around to see if anyone noticed anything last night?' Culley said. 'Anyone hanging round the *Brianna*, men on the quay whom no one recognized.'

'Do that.' Newton nodded. 'I'm supposed to meet the superintendent at nine.'

'I'll make a start after breakfast,' Culley said.

He beckoned to the waiter and held up the empty toast rack.

'Scotland Yard is paying for this, isn't it?'

*   *   *

As soon as Newton closed his hotel-room door behind him, he knew someone had been in there. The suitcase which he left under the window had been moved yet the bed was unmade. For a second he assumed that the chambermaid had begun to tidy and been called away. He slipped a comb out of his pocket and opened the wardrobe door to check himself in the mirror ready for his appointment with Rawle. As the reflection moved across the room, he caught sight of a wicker basket on the far side of the bed.

With half a thought that this was something to do with the chambermaid's work, instinct made Newton cross the room to check. Leaning casually over the basket, he jumped back when he caught sight of what was inside: a baby, a few weeks old, months maybe; he had no idea. It was fast asleep. Newton stood bolt upright and stared. While the basket itself was old and broken in places, the infant was swaddled in a snowy blanket. There were two glass bottles stoppered with paper tucked down the side; one contained some clear liquid, the other milk.

The child lay perfectly still; its eyes were closed, the white blanket folded carefully over the top of its head. For a terrible moment, Newton thought it was dead. His hands shook as he reached down, picked up the basket and placed it on the bed. He stared at the tiny round face. The child did not move. Its eyes stayed glued shut; its lips were pressed together. The swaddling blanket meant he could see no rise and fall in its chest.

Newton leaned across the basket and put his cheek close to the child's face. Almost at once he felt a feather breath against his skin. At the same time, he caught a sweet sugary scent together with the smell of something bitter which he couldn't place. Relief swept through him. As he stood up, he noticed a sheet of folded paper which had been slipped behind the bottles. The writing was in a careful round hand, black ink on thin paper. It ran: *His name is Reuben*. Newton turned the paper over; there was nothing more.

Newton stepped back. Had someone deliberately planted this infant in his care? His indignation swelled into anger. How dare they? He sat down on the bed and stared into the basket. Who could have done this? He had been in the town hardly a day; no one knew him here. Was someone out to ruin him? Was the implication that the child was his? He visualized the look of contempt on Rawle's face when he told him; he would delight in filing a report for Scotland Yard. What would Culley pick up from local gossip? Then he shivered as if the window had let in a sudden draught. How would Abigail regard him now? To judge by the milk, the infant was not yet weaned.

Then Newton remembered the smell. He pulled out the bottle of clear liquid and slipped out the paper stopper. The sweet smell of sugar-water almost hid the faint, sharp scent of laudanum. That was why the child slept so deeply.

Downstairs, the reception desk was unattended; noise from the dining room meant that breakfast was underway. Newton rang the bell. The longer he was forced to wait, the more anger built inside him. The nerve of it: some hussy who tried to palm her bastard off on the first respectable man she saw; a girl from the quay too afraid to own up to what she had done; some serving girl dismissed from her post who remembered where the master keys were kept. He slapped his hand down on the bell again.

The manager, Mr Potter, was horrified. Immaculately dressed in black jacket and pinstripes, a calculated curl in the centre of his forehead and a trim moustache on his lip, he was used to pleasing the hotel guests; his face turned the colour of chalk.

'This morning, during breakfast?' Open-mouthed, he pressed the palms of his hands against his cheeks while he struggled to make sense of what Newton was telling him.

Newton beckoned him to follow. Potter scuttled after him up the stairs.

'You have absolutely no idea?' Potter said. 'You're quite positive? You heard nothing? Saw nothing?'

Newton ignored the flurry of questions. He flung open the bedroom door; there was Reuben in his basket, still fast asleep. Potter clutched at the wardrobe for support.

'I want this . . . ' Newton gestured towards the basket; he couldn't bring himself to say the word *child* ' . . . removed, now.'

'But I . . . ' Potter was at a loss.

The sounds from the dining room downstairs carried through the open door: breakfast-time conversation, the clatter of cutlery on china. Through the window they could hear sounds from the quay outside, shouts as the men went to work, the rattle of wagon wheels over the cobbles.

'Now,' Newton repeated, staring at Potter's ashen face.

Both men peered into the basket. The baby's eyes were tight shut.

'You have no idea . . . ?' Potter began.

'I believe he has been given laudanum,' Newton said. 'That is why he is sleeping so soundly.'

'He?' Potter looked ill.

Newton thrust the paper with the child's name into Potter's hand.

'I shall send for a constable.' It was all Potter could think of to say. Unable to take his eyes off the sleeping child, he pressed his fingertips to his cheeks again.

'The child needs a nurse not a constable,' Newton snapped. The man was hopeless. 'What about your staff? Chambermaids, cooks; who is in the building this morning? Could this . . . belong to any of them?'

Potter seemed to hear him for the first time.

'My staff are all of the highest calibre.' He puffed out his chest. 'I can assure you, we do not employ anyone with less than unimpeachable morals. I conduct the interviews and take up the references myself . . . '

'Who is working here this morning?' Newton had no time for this blather. The realization formed in his mind that he was going to have to stand in Superintendent Rawle's office and explain this.

'The waiters and kitchen staff. They are all men.' Panic sounded in Potter's voice. 'Mrs Gladwell, the cook, is on breakfasts this week. She is a mature lady. She has worked here for many years and I am quite certain . . . '

'If she is the only female employee on the premises, I require you to get her up here and give her charge of the child.' Newton had no time for Potter's rambling explanation. 'I have a nine o'clock appointment. When I return, I wish the infant to be gone. It is your responsibility. Do I make myself clear?'

★  ★  ★

The wall clock showed five minutes past nine as Newton strode into Rawle's office. The room still held its night-time cold; the ashes of the previous day's fire lay in the grate.

'You're late, Inspector.' Rawle was seated behind his desk; he did not get up. 'Please be on time in future.'

Newton bit his lip and said nothing.

'I have read the sergeant's logbook,' Rawle continued. 'Constable Lamb is newly appointed. It is clear that coming across the girl disturbed him badly. He did not know who she was. I shall deal with him personally as soon as he comes on duty today. It is most unfortunate that these events coincided with your

76

visit.' Rawle adjusted the papers on his desk. He barely looked up. 'As soon as Miss March is recovered, I imagine you will wish to proceed with the inspection of the rifles.'

Newton tried to decide whether Rawle was more worried about attracting the wrath of the Chief Constable because of the actions of one of his men or because a visiting dignitary had to be fished out of the Torridge.

'Regrettable as yesterday's events were,' Rawle sounded as though he was reading minutes, 'they cannot be laid at the door of the Borough Police.'

'Your constable threw a woman into the river at high tide.' Newton laughed. What excuse had Rawle dreamed up now?

'He was attacked.' Rawle's face was white; his voice shook. 'The woman broke his nose. He defended himself.'

His fingers felt for the pile of papers on his desk and squared them up.

'Miss March, I hardly need remind you, is under your protection not mine,' Rawle countered. 'What kind of woman throws herself into the river?' Rawle stared at Newton, his lips pressed in a thin smile.

'A brave one,' Newton said flatly.

'I run this station like a regulator clock, sir. All my men are literate; each makes a record of his watch in his own time and hands it to the sergeant at the start of his shift the following day. They are punctual and properly turned out; I instructed them in their duties myself.' He looked up at Newton. An angry blush crept above the collar of his uniform. 'I refute any implication that yesterday was the fault of this station.'

'Last night, a girl was murdered.' Newton's voice was cold. 'It is your responsibility to find the killer.'

'I do not need you to inform me of my duties.' The blush spread across Rawle's face. He got to his feet and faced Newton across his desk.

'You came down here to accompany a visitor from the Dominion who wished to see the cache of arms my men seized.' Rawle's self-control almost throttled him. 'Instead of which, the visitor, who incidentally turns out to be a woman, throws herself into the river and almost drowns. Were it not for the actions of the quick-thinking boatman who hauled her out, her body would be languishing under the arches of the bridge as we speak.'

'Your constable threw a woman into the water.' Newton took a pace forward. 'Miss March, with presence of mind and heroic courage which is rare for either sex, dived in and saved her. You should be grateful, or the man you appointed would be in a cell awaiting the noose.'

Rawle's hands moved across the desk, feeling for papers to arrange.

'More than likely, that young woman was the only witness,' Newton went on. 'She could have identified the gunrunners. The only evidence which remains is a wrecked boat with an Irish name.'

When Rawle spoke, his voice was matter-of-fact. Newton knew he wanted to get rid of him.

'I suggest you carry out your duties, Inspector, and leave me to carry out mine.' He stared down at his desk. 'I suggest you carry out your inspection and then make your way back to London.' He sat down and selected a sheet of paper from the top of one of the piles. 'Now, if you'll excuse me . . . '

★ ★ ★

Outside, hungry gulls screeched as they wheeled over the fishing boats. The shops at the lower end of the High Street were open but there were few people about. As Newton stomped off his irritation with Rawle, he caught sight of Culley walking towards him.

'The superintendent is giving you his full support, is he?' Culley laughed.

'He'll probably file a complaint,' Newton

said. 'No doubt it will be waiting for me at Scotland Yard.'

Culley relished a row between his superiors.

'Something happened this morning at the hotel.' Newton caught Culley by the arm; he had to tell him.

Culley listened wide-eyed as Newton went through the story of the baby.

'Someone's got it in for you, sir.'

'Some chambermaid,' Newton said. 'That's all it is. She saw a visitor from London. Down here they probably think everyone in London is a millionaire.'

Culley looked at him hard.

'Anything else you want to tell me?'

Newton knew what he meant but ignored it.

'What should there be?'

'You can trust me with this, sir. Wouldn't be the first time . . . '

Newton cut him short.

'There's nothing like that.'

Culley shrugged.

'If you say so, sir. We're men of the world, you and me. There's nothing you could say — '

'I assure you, Sergeant.' Newton glared at him.

'No one could have followed you down from London, could they?' Culley was like a terrier. 'To dump the baby on you far away from home. No one's reputation need suffer then.'

'Sergeant,' Newton snapped. 'I have told you. This is nothing personal.'

'Only, there was a woman on the train.'

'What?' Newton halted so abruptly, Culley cannoned into him.

'A woman carrying a child pushed past us on the station. She was travelling alone.'

Newton stared at him. He remembered a woman on the station platform; a veil covered her face.

'The porter saw her to a carriage.'

'I know, Sergeant.' Feeling as if someone had just pulled a chair from under him, Newton was furious. 'I remember.'

'It's just a starting point, sir. If you want to find out — '

'I don't want to find out anything. This has nothing to do with me. The wretched child may simply have been left in the wrong room for all I know.'

They were standing outside the door to the Newfoundland Inn. Up and down the quay, people were getting on with their lives. Men were working on the boats; women pushed past on their way to the high-street shops; a farm cart was having difficulty negotiating the turn on to the bridge.

'All right.' Newton pulled himself together. 'See what you can find out about this woman.'

'Right, sir.'

'And I don't want Miss March to know.' Newton watched Culley's face, but it gave nothing away. He stumbled over his words. 'What I mean is I may tell her in my own time. A matter such as this . . . '

'I understand, sir.' Culley's face was a mask.

'You may as well get on with that as anything. There's no point in looking over the fishing boat again. Now that the witness is dead, an investigation won't get anywhere. Our duty is now to ensure the safety of Miss March.' Mentioning her name, he felt warmth spread to his cheeks; he looked at Culley to see if he had noticed. 'As soon as she is sufficiently recovered, we shall arrange for her to inspect the damn rifles. Then we shall take the train.'

'I'll start with the carriage drivers,' Culley said. 'Someone must know where this woman is staying.'

★ ★ ★

As Culley made his way down the quay, Newton hammered on the door to the Newfoundland Inn. Bolts rattled across and Lizzie Hookway stood there. Her hair was

82

bunched under her mobcap, she wore a clean apron and her sleeves were rolled up. She stared fiercely at Newton; unwilling to let him in, she held the door ajar.

'I've taken her up porridge and eggs and made up the fire,' Lizzie Hookway said curtly. 'I've told her that after what she's been through, she should rest herself today. You needn't bother us again.'

Before she finished speaking, someone called her name from inside. As Newton pushed the door open, Abigail walked towards them from the foot of the stairs. The upturned collar of a long cape framed her pale face; a velvet scarf was wrapped round her neck and her hair was pinned up under a black straw hat.

'Now, miss, you shouldn't . . . '

'I have sufficiently recovered, Lizzie.' Abigail took Lizzie Hookway's hand and squeezed it gently. 'Thank you for your many kindnesses.'

Her skin was almost translucent; her voice caught in her throat. She smiled warmly at each of them.

'If it weren't for Lizzie, I should not be standing here now. She made up the fire last night and this morning. My breakfast was a feast.'

'I avoided toast,' Lizzie Hookway confided. 'Lest it catch in the throat.'

The compliments had made her glow.

'There, you see,' Abigail said. 'I was thoroughly spoiled and here I am. Have you come to take me to our viewing of the contraband, Inspector?'

Outside on the quay, Newton strolled at a gentle pace to allow Abigail to keep up.

'I must say, I am most glad to see you well.'

'I was never ill, Inspector.' A smile played at the corners of her mouth. 'Just a little cold from my swim and a little nauseous from a few mouthfuls of river water. Now tell me, did you find Catalin? There was a constable posted outside my room all night, but he knew nothing.'

'If we make our inspection now, we shall be in time for the noon train,' Newton said quickly. 'Your report to your father is our priority now that you are back on your feet.'

'I want to know about Catalin,' Abigail insisted.

'You said she spoke French,' Newton said. 'You were able to converse with her?'

'I speak French; not well, but enough for everyday purposes.' Abigail smiled modestly. 'My father says in the new Dominion we should all know both French and English. New Brunswick, Ontario, Quebec, the Northwest Territories — we are all one country now.'

'Your father must be a very progressive man.'

'He is.' Abigail smiled. 'Under Mr Mac-
Donald's government, he says we should
strive for the equality of all our people; men,
women and all nationalities. He is a believer
in the ideas of your Mr Mill. He says he will
strive to make the new Dominion an example
to the world.'

She looked at Newton as if she was trying
to gauge his reaction.

'He is an advocate of suffrage for women.
He has tabled motions in our parliament. It is
his belief that one day the rights of women
will be equal to those of men. It is my belief
too. Are you familiar with Mr Mill's work
*The Subjection of Women*, Inspector?'

Newton couldn't remember whether he
had heard of it.

' "The legal subordination of one sex to the
other is wrong in itself and is one of the chief
hindrances to human improvement . . . " '
Abigail recited the quotation as if it were a
poem. 'Do you not agree, Inspector?'

'I don't doubt . . . ' Newton was at a loss.
Ordinarily, when he heard the topic mentioned,
it appeared fanciful to him. Not that he was
against it, it was just that this insistence on
the equality of what he had been brought up
to believe were opposites seemed so strange
as to be impossible. But within his lifetime,
had not Mr Brunel built ships out of iron?

Whoever could have predicted that? And now when Abigail spoke of suffrage with such conviction, she made it sound like a truth which the world had not yet discovered; he could not find a way to disagree with her.

'Anyway.' Abigail caught his eye. 'Where is Catalin?'

When Newton told her, Abigail's pace did not falter; she kept her eyes fixed on some distant point further up the quay. Overhead, gulls cried out.

'Who is the suspect?' Her face was white. 'Has anyone been arrested?'

'It is the business of the Borough Police. We must concentrate on our inspection of the weapons,' Newton said. 'I have arranged it with the superintendent of police. You must make your observations and then we shall return to London. Your father will be expecting you.'

'I am a witness, surely.' Abigail turned towards him. 'The police may require me to give a statement. I may be of some use.'

'The matter is in the hands of the local superintendent,' Newton said. 'Should he see the need to interview you, I am sure he will do so.'

'It is wrong for us to return to London when we could be of some assistance here.' Abigail's voice fell to a whisper. 'The poor girl . . . '

'The investigation will be carried out by the local constables; they have begun their work.' Newton wanted to reassure her. 'I called on Superintendent Rawle this morning.'

'There are three of us,' Abigail said fiercely. 'You, an inspector with the Metropolitan Police, Mr Culley, a sergeant, and myself. We should offer to help. It is the least we can do.'

High colour rose in Abigail's cheeks. She stopped in her tracks.

'Miss March,' Newton insisted, 'I assure you this is a matter for the Borough Police.'

'Well, I do not agree.' She stared at Newton. 'I shall make this clear to my father when I submit my report.'

★   ★   ★

In the police station, the sergeant seemed to have trouble with the lock to the cell door. Rawle joined them for the inspection. He ignored Newton and greeted Abigail politely; he said he hoped she was no worse off for her ducking and complimented her on the prettiness of her scarf.

As far as Newton could tell, Abigail was resigned to the fact that after they had made their inspection, Culley would make arrangements for their luggage, they would take a carriage across the bridge and leave. On the short walk to the police station, Newton did his best to impress on her how necessary it was for both him and Culley to resume their duties in London. Abigail did not comment.

The sergeant succeeded in locking the cell door when he should have unlocked it and had to start again. Rawle cleared his throat loudly to cover the awkwardness. When the sergeant eventually swung open the heavy door, the cell was empty.

No one spoke. Rawle pushed past and stared in disbelief at the walls of the cell, as if the cases of rifles were there, but he just couldn't see them.

'Well?' Newton snapped.

'Five cases.' The words dried in the sergeant's throat. 'The constables shouldered 'em in. I locked the door myself.'

'Did you check on them last evening?' It was all Rawle could think of to say.

'Locked the door myself, sir,' the sergeant said.

'Who knew they were here?' Newton snapped.

'No one.' The sergeant's voice shook. 'Only the constables.'

'Were all the rifles stored here?' Abigail asked.

'Someone must have seen them carry the cases in,' Newton said.

'My men unloaded 'em on the skern before the boat was towed round to the quay. We borrowed the farmer's cart and transported 'em back from where the vessel ran aground.' The sergeant seemed dazed. 'We weren't taking any chances by unloading her in full view of the town.'

'Were all the rifles stored here?' Abigail asked again. 'None were kept elsewhere?'

'The men who towed her in knew,' the sergeant said.

'Who were they?' Newton said. 'Fishermen from the quay?'

'Superintendent,' Abigail insisted. 'Are there rifles in any other place or was the whole consignment stored here?'

'It was all here.' Rawle's face crumpled.

Abigail pulled her scarf tight; the damp air caught in her throat.

Rawle gestured them out of the cell and towards the stairs.

'When you tried to unlock the door just now, it was already unlocked,' Newton said. 'Where do you keep the keys?'

The sergeant held an iron hoop in his hand; two heavy keys were attached to it, one for each of the cells. He looked helplessly at Rawle.

'Where they're always kept. At the back of my desk.'

'And are there copies of these keys?' Abigail interrupted.

The sergeant caught Rawle's eye again, to find out whether he should answer.

'There's a spare in the drawer of the desk in the superintendent's office.'

'That's enough, Sergeant,' Rawle said. 'This is a concern of the Borough Police.' He turned to Newton. 'I believe your business here is now done, Inspector. The sergeant will arrange for a carriage to collect your luggage and conduct you all across the bridge to the station. I regret that the inspection was not possible. I shall make it my business to cable Scotland Yard as soon as the items are discovered.'

Rawle gestured for them to leave the cell again.

'Sergeant, as soon as you have shown our visitors out, send a runner to find the constables, night and day watch, and get them to report to me in one hour.'

'Superintendent.' Abigail touched Rawle's arm as he turned towards the stairs. 'I want to thank you for sparing time to be with us this morning. Even in our far-away Dominion, we are fighting the same enemy as you; our struggle is equally great. The purpose of my father's visit to this country is to cement the ties that bind our two nations in tackling a common foe.'

'Miss March.' Rawle stiffened his shoulders;

he was taken aback. 'I am glad we were able to be of service. But, if you will excuse me, I must return to my duties . . . '

'We are on the same side.' Abigail continued undeterred. 'You appreciate that Chief Inspector Gillis of Scotland Yard and Sir Lawrence Yare, to say nothing of a member of the Dominion parliament, are waiting for me to report to them. I shall say that the shipment of Fenian weapons went missing from a locked cell in a Borough Police station. I shall be obliged to add that this disappearance took place the day after a girl who sailed on the boat which carried them was murdered.' She turned to Newton. 'While an inspector of the Metropolitan Police and his sergeant stood by.'

'Miss March, I must insist.' Rawle's face froze 'You are aware that I have pressing matters . . . '

'These guns were to have been sent by my sergeant to London today,' Newton weighed in. 'Miss March is right, we are all concerned here. This business is the concern of the Metropolitan force, just as much as the Borough. With Miss March's permission, Sergeant Culley will telegraph Scotland Yard and say our return has been delayed. We shall remain and assist with the inquiry. You have complained that you are short-handed; Sergeant Culley and I will help to hurry your investigation along.'

Rawle turned his back on them and stamped up the stairs. Newton pursued him to his office.

'I have not asked for your help and I do not require it,' Rawle snapped. Red-faced, he stared at Newton across his desk. 'If you wish to join us, then join us. Just make sure you put in your report that you had the full cooperation of the Borough Police.'

'Two matters.' Newton would not be put off. 'Firstly, I am surprised to learn that you allow your constables to frequent public houses in the town.'

'What are you saying?' Rawle's face hardened. The nerve of the man; what gave this Metropolitan inspector the right?

'My sergeant came upon your Constable Lamb drinking in the Newfoundland Inn last evening. Apparently, the drink made him garrulous. He entertained the clientele with the story of how he threw the girl off the boat.'

'And what was your sergeant doing in there?' Rawle scoffed. 'Does the great Scotland Yard permit its sergeants to visit drinking dens?'

Newton ignored him.

'Lamb went on to tell everyone how he would like to deal with the poor girl.'

'Poor girl? The harpie who broke his nose?'

Rawle sat down. 'Is that the poor girl you are referring to?'

'My sergeant heard him say that he wished he had cut the girl's throat.'

'What are you suggesting?' Rawle articulated each word distinctly. His voice dropped to a whisper; his eyes blazed.

'In front of witnesses,' Newton concluded.

'This is outrageous.' Rawle exploded. His hands felt for papers on his desk. 'If you wish to level an accusation against one of my constables, you better have hard evidence, Inspector, not public-house tittle-tattle.'

'And for your information, my sergeant followed the man to the Newfoundland Inn in the course of his enquiries.' Newton remembered the smell of whiskey on Culley's breath. 'Metropolitan officers and constables are prohibited from frequenting public houses.'

'Constable Lamb will be submitting his account of the incident on the boat when he arrives this morning; his memorandum will speak for itself.'

Rawle turned to the papers on his desk.

'If there is nothing else . . . '

He pulled a document towards him and made a show of becoming engrossed in his work.

'Close the door behind you, Inspector.'

Rawle did not look up. 'The fire is not yet lit.'

Newton did not move.

'And I have not yet finished.'

Rawle slapped down the paper he was reading. This inspector was arrogant and overbearing; like all those working in the capital, he had no comprehension of the difficulties which faced him and his small force of Borough Police.

'What more do you wish to say?' Rawle gritted his teeth. The only crumb of comfort left to him was that he would be sure to record all this in due course in his daily memorandum.

'Your sergeant met me at the quay last night.'

'On my instructions,' Rawle said. 'I am well aware he came to the quay.'

'And you asked him to pass on the message that you had gone to inspect the watch and would see me at nine this morning.'

Rawle failed to see where this was leading.

'Superintendent.' Newton stared at him. 'That left your station unmanned. Did your sergeant lock up before he left for the quay?' He didn't wait for an answer. 'I think not. He told me the night watch were on their patrols and he was about to return to lock the station for the night before joining you and then making his way home.'

Rawle pushed his chair sharply back from his desk.

'Most likely, the police station was being watched and it is due to the negligence of your sergeant that the arms were stolen.'

'You should not be the one to cast a stone.' Rawle jumped to his feet; papers scattered across his desk. 'It is exacting work that my men do.' His hands shuffled agitatedly amongst the papers. 'If you had kept proper watch over Miss March you would have prevented her from launching herself into the river. No thanks to you, we escaped a tragedy.' His anger boiled over. 'Whose ludicrous idea was it to send a woman down to inspect a shipment of arms? She is from the colonies, the daughter of some tin-pot parliamentarian. I ask you. How in God's name can she write a report?'

'If you knew Miss March as well as I do,' Newton countered, 'you would understand that no one in the world can prevent her from doing anything she sets her mind to.'

'Thank you, inspector.' It was Abigail's voice. She stood in the doorway to the office.

'Superintendent, I can assure you that the new Dominion parliament which governs a country many times the size of this one is anything but tin-pot.' She smiled generously. 'And I can also assure you, having studied medical science for many years, even though I am not yet permitted a practitioner's licence because of my sex, I am very good at writing reports.'

# 6

Later the same day, Abigail and Newton walked the length of the quay. The morning was bright and a sharp wind blew off the river. The fishermen hunkered down behind whatever shelter they could find; carters walked in the lee of their wagons; scurrying pedestrians pulled their coats tight to their throats. Beneath the bay windows of the Newfoundland Inn, the benches were empty.

Newton's thoughts slipped back to the baby in his hotel room. There was no need for Abigail to know about this. While he felt uncomfortable keeping this from her, the thought of having to explain such a thing was intolerable; innocent as he was, he would hardly know where to begin. It was a slur on his character and he wanted her to think well of him. Even if their stay in the town was longer than they had intended, he should be able to make sure the child was spirited away to be taken care of by the proper authorities, whoever they were. The hotel manager would be the last person to broadcast the news. No doubt, he would have to deal with whatever sly imputation Rawle came up with. But that was different; facing down the superintendent would be no problem.

'All the time we were in Lizzie's upstairs room, Catalin gripped the sheets until her knuckles were white.'

The wind had stung colour into Abigail's cheeks, although her lips were still pale.

'I thought it was a reaction, from the shock of being in the river.'

'If it hadn't been for your courage — ' Newton began.

Abigail didn't let him finish.

'The poor girl was terrified. Even though the fire was lit and Lizzie was waiting on us, Catalin talked about getting back to the boat as soon as she opened her eyes.'

Abigail pulled the scarf tight around her neck and folded her arms under her cape.

'This is a sea wind,' Newton said cautiously. He feared that if he made a direct suggestion that they return indoors, she would reject it outright. 'The quayside is exposed.'

Abigail turned and looked back along the moorings.

'I should arrange for your trunk to be moved to the hotel,' Newton continued. 'The rooms are spacious and quite comfortable.'

'Out of the question.' Abigail sounded surprised that he should suggest such a thing.

'Lizzie has taken wonderful care of me. I shall certainly not move from here.'

'But the inn . . . ' Newton floundered. 'The noise from the downstairs parlour. The room is . . . '

'More than adequate,' Abigail said flatly. 'I should not dream of moving. Lizzie has befriended me and I am fond of her.'

At the far end of the quay, Rawle's men began their search. A group of constables stood talking to the fishermen working on their nets while their colleagues swarmed over the boats and lowered themselves into the holds. Culley stood slightly apart, keeping watch, eavesdropping on their conversations.

'They won't find anything,' Newton said dismissively. 'No skipper will set sail until the wind drops; beyond the headland, the seas must be raging. If someone wanted to ship the rifles out, they would hold back from loading until the vessel was ready to put to sea.'

An argument broke out between the constables and a group of fishermen who clearly resented the intrusion on their boat. A line of men stood in the way to prevent the constables from boarding. As they squared up to the constables, Culley stepped in to mediate.

'Anyone would guess Rawle would search

the moorings,' Newton continued. 'It is the obvious place.'

'The superintendent could hardly not search the boats.' Abigail smiled at him.

'A discreet watch on the quay would have been more effective,' Newton insisted. 'This is Rawle's show of strength. He wishes everyone to see a search in progress. He intends it to frighten the Fenians or smugglers or whoever they are into the belief that they cannot succeed.'

'And you are convinced this will merely make them more secretive.' Abigail held her hat in place against a sudden gust of wind.

'The temperature has fallen,' Newton said.

'Perhaps we should return indoors,' Abigail said. 'We could keep watch from the window of the inn.'

Abigail took a last look along the quay, anxious not to miss anything. Culley had his arm round the shoulder of one of the fishermen and was explaining something intently to him; the constables had their billy clubs in their hands.

'Sergeant Culley will be our eyes and ears,' Newton assured her.

As soon as Newton and Abigail settled themselves beside the blazing fire in the parlour bar of the Newfoundland Inn, Lizzie Hookway scuttled over with glasses of hot brandy and ginger on a tray. She told Abigail off for spending time outside.

'You ain't used to it, miss. These westerlies lift the cold right off the water.'

'My dear, it is so kind of you to be concerned for me.' Abigail tutted. 'Fresh air is good for the constitution and does wonders for the brain. Besides that, at home most of the country is covered in snow right now.'

Lizzie Hookway looked horrified. 'You have to look after yourself, that's all I'm saying.'

Abigail laughed. 'Your fire is wonderful. I shall soon be as warm as toast.'

'If you don't mind me asking, miss.' There was clearly something on Lizzie Hookway's mind. 'I've lived across the quay from that river for forty years; nothing would persuade me to jump in there. Where did you learn to swim like that?'

'A river runs through my grandfather's farm. When we were children, it was where my sisters and I spent our summers. Every winter the river is iced over, but after the spring thaw, it's beautiful. My sisters and I spent whole days by the river when we were girls.'

Lizzie Hookway struggled to visualize someone swimming in a river which was frozen all winter.

'We all used to swim there,' Abigail went

on. 'My father taught us when we were quite young.'

'I shouldn't like it.' Lizzie Hookway shook her head. 'The colonies wouldn't suit me at all. Wild horses couldn't drag me to swim in a river.'

'Once you have learned to stay afloat, swimming is a most carefree pastime,' Abigail insisted. 'The exercise is good for the limbs.'

Lizzie Hookway's eyes widened. She placed the brandies on the table and hurried off.

Entranced by Abigail's good-natured candour, Newton struggled to bring his thoughts back to the present. For a second, he considered acknowledging his discovery of finding the infant, but something inside him prevented him.

'Did the girl, Catalin, say anything else?' Newton said, returning to police business.

'She said the constable ordered her to leave the boat.' Abigail loosened the buttons on her cape. 'She refused because she had nowhere to go. He dragged her out of the hold. She struggled with him on deck.'

'And was that when you arrived?' Newton said.

'At that exact moment.'

'And if I'd been a minute quicker, I would have prevented you from jumping into the river,' Newton said.

'Can you swim, Inspector?'

'I cannot.' Newton raised his chin above his collar to make himself sound exaggeratedly pompous and English. 'And neither can I fly. Until I met you, Miss March, I never considered either a disadvantage.'

Abigail rocked with laughter; her face lit up. Newton loved to see it; he blushed that he was able to affect her like this.

'And you never wanted to?' Abigail's eyes sparkled. 'Swim, I mean; flying is for the birds.'

'Never.' Newton maintained his pretence of aloofness; he began to relish her teasing him.

Abigail sipped her brandy and stared out of the window.

'Did Catalin say how she came to be on the boat?' Newton was serious again.

'There were marks on her wrists,' Abigail said. 'Rope burns. I saw them as plain as day.'

'She'd been tied?' Newton's voice sounded hollow.

'Until recently; in places the skin was broken.' Abigail stared at him. 'The superintendent is concerned to search for missing boxes of rifles. Will he put the same energies in to tracking down the murderer of poor Catalin?'

Newton excused himself and went to the window to check on Culley.

Abigail's forthrightness disturbed him. As a Metropolitan Police inspector, Newton prided himself on his ability to look life in the face. He had spent time with murderers, wife-beaters and individuals whose twisted natures rendered them only fit for the asylum; on the streets of the capital, he had witnessed the worst aspects of human nature. He was brave; his physical courage had been tested many times. He had a steely morality: he had turned down offers of bribes which would have made him wealthy. He upheld the values of law and order and never wavered from his duty. Yet for some reason, this young woman's confident assertions found him unguarded.

What made the privileged daughter of a Member of Parliament on a visit from the Dominion concerned about the death of a sailor's whore? What was the instinct which possessed her to pitch herself into a flood tide to save someone she didn't know? Even in the regiment where men showed extraordinary courage, Newton had met no one like this.

Abigail affected Lizzie Hookway, too. Newton saw it all too clearly. She was fussing over Abigail now, trying to persuade her to take a blanket for her knees. Abigail laughed and protested that Lizzie spoilt her more than she had ever been used to. She took the blanket with effusive thanks. Lizzie Hookway's face shone with affection.

Abigail found a way of making each person she spoke to feel unique, Newton reflected. Tough Lizzie Hookway who spent her days rousting drunken fishermen off the premises became gentleness itself; Catalin, too terrified to speak to anyone, had confided in her. There was more than that, though: her physical strength in withstanding the cold of the river, her courage, the quickness of mind with which she stripped out the bones of every conversation made her quite unlike anyone he had ever met.

The brandy burned Newton's throat. As he stared into the fire, he felt the liquor enter his head and make his thoughts slide. When he'd encountered notions of women's suffrage in the past, he'd scoffed. Such ideas seemed fantastical, a dreamed-up philosophy with no grounding in the hard reality he was used to. But here was Abigail, who had studied to become a doctor and at the end of her studies was denied a licence to practise because she was a woman. The world, he decided, was on its head.

'Inspector.' Abigail called him back from his reverie. 'Lizzie is asking if you require more brandy.'

'No.' Newton smiled. 'Thank you. I have a question though. Last night, Constable Lamb was in here. Did you speak to him?'

'John Lamb? No I did not,' Lizzie Hookway snapped. 'I've turfed him out of here enough times. He's a troublemaker from a family of troublemakers. When there's drink inside him his fists start swinging. Heaven knows what possessed them to make him a constable.'

'Did you hear anything he said?' Newton carried on.

'His father used to come in here when he first brought his family up from Cornwall to work on the lime kilns. They went home when the work dried up. They've been back here for a few months now,' Lizzie Hookway said. 'He behaved himself last night, though. He was drinking with your sergeant; that's who he spent the evening with.'

Newton announced he wished to ride out to see for himself where the *Brianna* had been washed ashore. Abigail brushed aside his concerns for her well-being and forbade him from leaving her behind. She merely requested time to rest and change.

While Abigail was upstairs, Culley pushed open the inn door.

'Tracked her down, sir.'

He slipped into the seat beside Newton.

'Last night she was booked in at the Royal Hotel, the other end of the bridge.'

'Have you seen her?' Newton suddenly

wanted to move away from the fire. 'Did you see the child?'

'She's gone. Asked for an early breakfast; the hall porter ordered her a carriage.'

'What about the child?'

'The porter couldn't actually say. He remembers her holding a basket. He didn't know what was in it.'

'What does he remember?' Newton was exasperated.

'It was 6.30 in the morning, sir. The porter's an old man; he'd been up all night.'

'What was her name?'

'Mrs Smith,' Culley said. 'I saw the register.'

'That's all?' Newton stared at him. 'Nobody knows anything else about her? What about the carriage driver?'

'No one's seen him. The porter said she's never stayed at the Royal before.' Culley hesitated. 'We were in the dining room at seven o'clock this morning, sir.'

'What are you suggesting?'

'I'm saying the time fits; it's possible she could have entered the hotel while we were at breakfast. That's all.'

Newton was aware that Culley was studying his reaction to all this, but Newton felt only genuine puzzlement. Why was his room chosen when he had been in the town less than twenty-four hours?

'I returned to our hotel,' Culley went on. 'The manager is convinced the reputation of the place will go to rack and ruin and no one will stay there ever again. He blames the staff, blames the guests, blames anyone who comes down from London.'

'Blames me?' Newton said. 'I can imagine it.'

'A constable has been summoned; all he's doing is standing in the hotel kitchen trying to look important. The vicar's been sent for as well; apparently he's on the Board of Guardians.'

'Where is the child now?'

'In the kitchen under the care of the cook and being cooed over by the chambermaids whenever they come on duty.'

'No one saw anyone with a baby in the hotel this morning, I take it.'

'That's right, sir.'

'Room keys?'

Culley shook his head.

'All the keys are kept at the front desk; staff, guests, everyone knows that. Anyone coming in from outside would know.' Culley did his best to reassure him. 'I shouldn't worry about it, sir. The Guardians will make sure the child is looked after; this will blow over.'

'Who else is staying there?'

'For what it's worth, I made a list from the register,' Culley said. 'Married couples. Commercial travellers. No one stands out.'

★ ★ ★

That afternoon, Abigail and Newton rode out to the salt marsh where the *Brianna* had run aground. A mile outside town, they picked up a cart track which led to a ridge of grey cobbles on the edge of the sea. The skern was desolate; it lay flat, deserted and beaten by the wind under a vacant sky. Marram grass clung to the edges of the dunes; storksbill, fescue and patches of sea blite carpeted the sandy ground; ribbons of eel grass waved in the bottom of the salt pools. Overhead, grey clouds hurtled inland; gulls screamed, bent double against the wind.

Inshore, the sea boiled. Cross-currents heaved the tide back and forth; each time a wave crashed, an undertow clawed at the sand and loaded the breakers with shingle. Along the tide line, driftwood and jetsam were strewn amongst the bladder-wrack. Offshore, an explosion of surf along the sand bar marked the frontier between the estuary and the open sea. Further out, white veins ruptured the surface where a stinging wind broke the swell. There was no way the vessels from the quay could put to sea in this.

Newton tethered the two hired ponies to a gorse bush. Abigail waved away the hand Newton held out to support her; she held her hat with one hand and gathered her skirt above her ankles with the other. She picked her way with care.

'Is this the place?' She had to shout against the wind.

Newton pointed to pieces of broken mast amongst the seaweed; he picked up lengths of rigging to show her. They hoped for something which would provide a link to the *Brianna*, a packing case perhaps, some of the crew's possessions. Walking side by side, they combed the sand, but found nothing.

Newton wanted to be able to visualize the events as they'd happened: the storm-tossed craft dragging her mast in the water hurled on to the sand; the crew wading through the breakers, desperate to be safe and ashore. Why had Catalin stayed on board? What made her afraid to leave the vessel, even as she foundered?

'The *Brianna* was trying to steer for the estuary, I take it,' Abigail said.

'Without a mast, she was at the mercy of the elements,' Newton said. 'If the coast had been rocky, she would have broken up.'

A rider approached from further along the pebble ridge. His black jacket had been patched and repaired many times; his old waistcoat was buttoned tight and a kerchief was knotted at his throat. Some of the buttons from his canvas gaiters were missing. His tousled hair and his side whiskers were steel grey; scoured by wind and rain, his face was the colour of raw meat. An old-fashioned flintlock musket lay across his saddle.

'Knew you wasn't Gypsies.' The man was suspicious. 'Those are hired ponies.'

Newton told him who they were.

'What are you after? Only I've had Gypsies out here. Keeping an eye out to make sure they don't come back.'

'Taking a look at the sight of the wreck,' Newton said.

'Policeman?' The farmer squinted at him. 'I had Superintendent Rawle and his constables crawling all over the place. He comes out here the minute some ketch gets blown ashore; he won't send a single man to help me shift the Gypsies.'

'This is a beautiful piece of land,' Abigail said admiringly.

'Three of my sheep drowned out here in that storm; the whole skern was neck deep,' the farmer said abruptly. 'What's your interest out here, miss?'

'I rode out with the inspector,' Abigail said warmly. 'I have never visited this part of the country.'

The farmer turned to Newton.

'Inspector, is it?' He shifted the musket over his saddle. 'James Molland. This is my land.'

'Are wrecks a common occurrence, Mr Molland?' Abigail smiled at him. 'On this stretch of the coast?'

'I wouldn't say common. A mile or two farther down towards Hartland, it's a different matter.' Molland pointed. 'Other side of the woods.'

South of where they stood, the ground rose sharply; the trees grew bent in half under the onslaught of the wind.

'My boundary stops at the trees. I set my fires along here.'

'Fires to warn the ships?' Abigail said.

Molland turned to Newton.

'Pert as a magpie, ain't she?' He laughed. 'Always asking questions.'

'Well, Mr Molland.' Abigail joined in the laughter. 'If you want to know something, the best way to find out is to ask.'

'We light fires when there's a storm blowing in to guide the vessels away from the point.'

'You do a great service, Mr Molland,' Abigail said.

Newton guessed what her next question was going to be. He watched Molland's surliness melt away as Abigail charmed answers out of him.

'Was there a fire on the night of the wreck?' Abigail said. 'Perhaps the storm was so thick, the sailors were unable to see it.'

'They could see it all right, if it was lit,' Molland said grimly.

'So you didn't light it?' Abigail pressed him.

'Lit it like I always do, three tar barrels. Wind, rain, nothing won't blow them out.'

'But the boat broke her mast, so she was driven on shore anyway,' Newton said. 'It didn't matter whether she'd seen a warning fire or not.'

'It didn't matter that someone put the fire out,' Molland said. 'When I couldn't see it from the house, I rode out here. The wind was so wild, it was as much as I could do to keep my horse from bolting. First thing I found was someone had dug a pit, upended the barrels and piled earth over 'em. The boat was carried halfway up the skern. The crew was long gone.'

'You're saying someone tried to lure the ship on to shore.' Newton wanted to be sure he'd understood correctly.

'Gypsies, I told Rawle. I rode into town to

113

let him know what had gone on. Soon as he knew there was a wreck, he was out here with his constables in no time.'

'Did he find who had done it?' Abigail said.

'Wasn't interested. All he cared about was leaving his men to guard the wreck and arranging to tow her in to the quay as soon as the storm blew itself out. Borrowed my cart to offload the cargo.'

'Why doesn't the superintendent move these Gypsies out if they're a trouble to you?' Newton said.

'Flat-out denies they even exist.' Molland's mouth tightened. 'Sent one of his constables out here to look for 'em once when I kept on at him. 'Course, he didn't find nothing. I told him they've been back here three months at least.' He leaned down from the saddle to make sure they didn't mistake his point. 'What he thinks is if he leaves 'em be, chances are they'll stay out here — away from the town there is much less for them to thieve. If they got into town then he'd have to get his constables to do something about them.'

After Molland wheeled his horse back in the direction he had come, Newton insisted he and Abigail follow the pebble ridge parallel to the sea. When they came to the barrels, it was just as Molland told them: three tar barrels, upended and half-buried in the sandy soil. Further on, where the ground rose and a stand of trees grew bent with the force of the wind, there was evidence of a camp. Saplings were cut back; a circle of burned earth showed where a fire had been; hoof prints and wagon tracks criss-crossed in the mud. From here nothing obscured the view over the flat marsh to the estuary mouth. They could even make out the place where the barrels were overturned. Further on down the coast, the chimney of a disused lime kiln jutted up close to a steep sea inlet; beyond that the roof of an isolated cottage was just visible. When they turned and looked back, they could see the mossy thatch of Molland's farmhouse in the lee of a fall in the land.

# 7

When Newton and Abigail returned to the Newfoundland Inn, Culley was waiting for them.

'This came for you.'

He handed Newton a telegram.

'It's from Gillis. He has received our wire and he wants a progress report.' Newton crumpled the sheet of paper and shoved it in his pocket. 'That means Sir Lawrence is breathing down his neck.'

'The constables've completed the search of the boats,' Culley said. 'They didn't find anything.'

Lizzie Hookway appeared and set down bowls of hot broth and hunks of bread in front of them. She fussed over Abigail, but had to admit that the ride had brought colour to her cheeks.

'I had a visit from the vicar.' Lizzie Hookway sniffed. 'First time he's deigned to set foot in here. He was looking for you, Inspector. He wanted you to know that the funeral service will be at noon tomorrow.'

Newton asked her about Gypsies.

'What Gypsies? They're here autumn-fair

week. Don't see hide nor hair of 'em the rest of the year.'

'What about recently?' Newton pressed her.

He told her about the campsite they had discovered out at Molland's farm.

'Some folk point the finger at Gypsies.' Lizzie Hookway leaned over him. 'When they don't know who else to blame.'

After finishing her broth, Abigail announced that she would retire to her room to rest. Ordinarily, she insisted, she never slept during the day, but said she felt that she had not yet fully recovered her strength.

'She looks well,' Culley volunteered, after Abigail had made her way upstairs.

'She has a strong constitution.' Newton felt warmth spring to his face at having to speak about Abigail in her absence. 'After yesterday, we should be grateful for it.'

'I could find one of the constables and ask if the night watch has reported any Gypsies in town,' Culley suggested. 'They open up to me if they're out of sight of the superintendent.'

Newton wanted to talk to the men who towed the *Brianna* from where she had run aground.

'The crew of the *Snowdrop*,' Culley said. 'They took a dinghy out at high tide and towed her in.'

The weather had worsened: rain threatened and clouds fled across a dirty sky; a lone gull struggled against the wind. The tide was now running out fast. Eddies and whirlpools pockmarked the glassy surface of the water; whole branches from upstream careered under the arches of the bridge and past the quay. The fishing boats shifted at their moorings. Without some further change in the weather, they would not be able to put out even when the tide turned: the skippers knew the sea beyond the mouth of the estuary. The quay was deserted. The men who were not crammed into the smoky parlour of the Newfoundland Inn went home until the weather broke.

As Culley led the way to the *Snowdrop*'s mooring, a constable hurried towards them down the quay. He clung on to his hat with one hand and waved furiously with the other.

'The superintendent asks that you come to his office.'

Constable Lamb skidded to a halt in front of Newton. The hobnails in his boots clattered on the cobbles.

'He asked me tell you it was important, sir.' Lamb's face reddened. 'And that he wishes you to come right away.'

Newton stared at him.

'Constable, have you written up your

memorandum on the events on the quayside yesterday?'

'Yes, sir.' Lamb's eyes darted nervously to Culley. 'Handed it in at the start of the morning shift like always.'

As they turned in the direction of the police station, Newton kept pace with the constable.

'I hear you are a patron of the Newfoundland Inn, Constable.'

'Sir?' Lamb kept his eyes straight ahead.

'In the Metropolitan force, we policemen are not permitted to make use of public houses situated in the area of our work.'

When they reached Rawle's office door, Newton rapped and entered without waiting for an answer. The air was comfortably warm from the coals in the grate; a gust of wind outside swept rain against the window.

'Inspector.' Rawle looked up from his desk, pen in hand.

He glanced at the vacant chairs which faced his desk, but did not invite Newton to sit. Culley hung back in the doorway.

'This is a private conversation, Sergeant.' Rawle stood up abruptly and crossed the room to the office door. 'Wait downstairs at the front desk, if you please.'

He edged the door closed almost before Culley had time to get out of the way.

'I have done you a great service, Inspector,' Rawle said. 'I have closed the case. I suggest you take the evening train, put up in Exeter overnight and continue on to Paddington in the morning.'

Newton was stunned.

'Your presence here is no longer necessary. You are free to go.'

Rawle sat down behind his desk and let his fingers run along the blade of a paperknife.

'I shall let the Metropolitan force know in due course.' Rawle raised his eyebrows as though he was surprised Newton was still standing there. 'I wished to tell you myself, as a courtesy.'

'You have apprehended the girl's murderers and recovered the rifles?' Newton couldn't hold back.

'There is another matter.' Rawle ignored the question. 'It has been reported to me that a child was found in your hotel room this morning.' Rawle paused. 'A babe in arms, torn from its mother's breast.'

Rawle's face was stone; he held up his hand to stop Newton from answering.

'The Reverend Dauncy considered it his duty to report this to me. He came into town to seek you out and discovered from the keeper of the Newfoundland Inn that you had gone riding with Miss March.'

'I asked the manager of the hotel to deal with this — ' Newton began.

'Do you fail to realize how rumour spreads?' Scarlet patches like insect stings appeared on Rawle's cheeks. 'Your good name is in tatters and the longer you are here, the more you endanger the reputation of this department. Do you expect me to believe that the wretched infant was placed in your hotel room within a day of your arrival by accident?'

Newton felt his hands clench into fists.

'What you are implying is scurrilous.' Newton did his best to keep all emotion out of his voice. 'I have no connection with this child. I do not know how it came to be there. My reputation is intact because my conscience is clear.'

'Then you have apprised Miss March of the situation, I presume?' Rawle picked up the paperknife and examined the blade as if he were looking for a speck of dirt.

'Of course I have not,' Newton snapped; he felt anger boil inside him.

'You were entrusted to safeguard the welfare of a diplomatic visitor by a chief inspector at Scotland Yard.' Rawle replaced the knife carefully on the desk. He looked up as if he was having to explain something to someone who did not understand. 'There is an implication here, Inspector. And that implication makes you unfit to carry out this responsibility. I have sent a telegram to Chief Inspector Gillis and requested the removal of your rank. I require you to have no further contact with my force of Borough Police; we shall complete the investigation without the assistance of either you or your Irish sergeant.'

'I have told you.' Newton was pale with fury. 'I have no connection with that child or any other, for that matter. If you continue with this slander, I shall bring an action against you for defamation of character.'

Rawle pushed back his chair and climbed to his feet. Leaning forward, he pressed the tips of his fingers on his desk until the knuckles were white.

'You seriously believe there is a judge in all the land who would rule in your favour, an individual of questionable morality who attacks the superintendent of police for fighting to uphold the good name of his borough force?' Rawle's voice shook. 'You are contemptible, Inspector. And your threat is empty.'

'Miss March wishes to attend the funeral of the girl tomorrow morning.' Newton stood his ground. 'If the investigation is completed, we shall take the London train after that.'

Rawle sat down again. His fingers moved towards the paperknife. He wanted the man out of his sight. Now that he had agreed to go, short of having his sergeant hurl him down the stairs, there was no more to be done.

'Tell me about the murderers,' Newton persisted. 'I am required to write a report.'

'Murderer.' Rawle corrected him; he was quick to take the opportunity to describe his success. 'Constable Lamb arrested a young ruffian on the quay this morning. He was found with a knife tucked in his belt which once belonged to the murdered girl. He confessed to cutting her throat.'

'Confessed?'

'Freely.' Rawle's stare was ice. 'There was no need for the constables to take stern measures in the cells.'

Newton waited.

'The man is a vagabond, known throughout the town. This arrest will come as no surprise to anyone,' Rawle said.

'And the guns?'

'My men have conducted a thorough search of the moorings; they will begin combing the skern at first light tomorrow. It is the obvious place,' Rawle said.

He leaned back in his chair.

'I suggest you instruct Miss March to see to her packing tonight. A carriage can take you to the station straight from the funeral. There will be no need for you to return to the town.'

'I wish to speak to the accused,' Newton said. 'What is his name?'

'The man has been charged, Inspector. He will be delivered to Exeter gaol tomorrow morning to await trial at the crown court.'

'I shall ask your sergeant to unlock the cell on my way out,' Newton said curtly.

'If you must, Inspector.' Rawle sighed. He was doing his utmost to remain civil; his face held a thin smile. 'Do not expect to get much out of him.'

'What time do you expect your men to return with the rifles?'

'Tomorrow evening,' Rawle said patiently. 'Once they have located the spot, I expect the digging to take no time at all.'

Downstairs at the sergeant's desk, Newton demanded he and Culley be taken down to the cells.

'His name's Edward Rumsam.' The sergeant shook his head sadly. 'He is well known to us, sir. I can't say this sorry business has come as a surprise.'

Rumsam jumped to his feet when the key clattered in the lock. He backed away from Newton, white-faced and terrified. He was a boy, fifteen or sixteen years old, tousle-haired and thin. He wore a torn shirt and trousers held up with farm twine; he was barefoot. Dirt ingrained the skin of his hands and face;

he stank of horse manure and fish.

'Sit down, Edward, the gentlemen ain't come to harm you.' The sergeant spoke matter-of-factly.

Rumsam's eyes darted from Newton to Culley. He snatched up a crust of bread which had lain beside him on the wooden bench and hid it in his folded arms.

'Do as the sergeant says,' Newton said.

Rumsam backed into the corner of the cell and sat hunched on the bench; an empty tin mug lay at his feet.

'You are accused of murder, Edward,' Newton began. 'What have you got to say about that?'

Rumsam's eyes filled with terror. He drew in his shoulders, hunched over and stared at the floor. He seemed to want to speak, but words stuck in his throat.

'Tell me, Edward,' Newton demanded.

As Newton took a step forward, Rumsam pulled his feet up and with the crust still in his hand, hugged his legs close to him. He peeped at Newton over the top of his knees. His voice was a whisper.

'Sir, let me . . . '

The sergeant pushed forward, but Newton grabbed his arm and held him back.

'I want to talk to you, Edward,' Newton insisted. 'Nothing more.'

'Sit up when the inspector is addressing you,' the sergeant barked.

Rumsam flinched and tightened his grip around his shins.

'Sergeant,' Newton interrupted before the sergeant could snarl at him again. 'Be so good as to bring the wretch a drink of water. That might encourage him to talk.'

'He's had his ration, sir.' The sergeant drew himself up. 'Superintendent Rawle orders one quarter-pint of water and four ounces of bread, morning and evening. He insists the prisoners are well looked after, sir.'

'That's as maybe, Sergeant,' Newton said patiently. 'I am requesting you to bring a cup of water at this time.'

As soon as the sergeant's footsteps echoed on the stone stairs, Newton began again.

'I am an inspector from the Metropolitan Police in London, Edward.' His tone was kindly. 'I wish to know what you have to say for yourself, that's all.'

Culley moved forward.

'Sir, do you wish me to . . . '

Newton held him back.

'This is my sergeant. Neither of us is here to hurt you.'

Rumsam watched him from behind his knees.

'You are on a serious charge, Edward. You

could hang for it. What have you got to say?'

Even with his legs hugged to him, Rumsam shivered. Newton could not tell if it was cold from the walls of the cell or fear.

'You were in possession of a knife, Edward.' Newton tried again. 'They claim you used it to cut the throat of a girl. You must have something to say for yourself.'

The sergeant's boot heels clicked on the stairs.

'Here you are, Edward.' He held out the mug of water.

Rumsam snatched it and gulped it down.

'Been talkative, has he?' the sergeant said.

'Not as yet,' Newton said.

'That's because you're not talking about the right thing, sir.' The sergeant grinned. 'The inspector's not asking you about seagulls, is he, Edward?'

Behind his knees, Rumsam shook his head violently.

'Where are the seagulls, Edward?' the sergeant continued.

Rumsam stared up at the ceiling and pointed, drawing an arc in the air.

'That's right,' the sergeant said. 'And where were the seagulls when you had that knife tucked in your belt, Edward?'

Rumsam pointed to all corners of the ceiling, a delighted smile on his upturned face.

'Where did you get the knife from?' Newton interrupted.

Rumsam ducked his head behind his knees again and tightened his arms round his shins.

'The inspector wants to know where the seagulls were when you picked up the knife,' the sergeant said.

Rumsam peered at him, then looked suspiciously at the others.

'You're a clever one, aren't you, Edward,' the sergeant laughed. 'You aren't going to let us catch you out like that, are you?'

A smile spread across Rumsam's face.

'See how he grins?' The sergeant laughed. 'Where were the seagulls when you cut the throat of that girl, Edward?' His voice became menacing. 'I'll wager they were circling overhead when you threw her poor body down into the hold.'

Rumsam buried his head behind his knees; the tin cup clattered on the floor.

'That's all you'll get for now.' The sergeant turned to Newton. 'He spends his days on the quay watching the gulls. That and thieving when he thinks he can get away with it.' He leaned forward. 'Ain't any seagulls in here, are there, Edward? When they send you down to Exeter, there won't be any gulls there, neither.'

Seeing there was no more to be gained,

Newton got to his feet. As the sergeant slammed the cell door shut behind them, Rumsam sat in the corner and hid his face.

'We picked him up with the bloodstained knife tucked in his belt, standing on the quayside, staring at the *Brianna*. They'll make short work of him at the assizes. The judge won't be asking where the seagulls were.'

'Why isn't he in the workhouse?' Culley said. 'He would have shelter and occupation.'

'The workhouse is full,' the sergeant said. 'Although that doesn't usually stop them from cramming in another one. It's because he's got somewhere to live. His parents are long dead, but his brother takes care of him. Somehow they scratch along.'

'So he's got someone to look after him?' Newton said.

'You will have seen his brother. You came by train, didn't you?'

'Westcott, the stationmaster?' Newton looked surprised.

'Not him, Inspector.' The sergeant chuckled. 'The boy who does his fetching and carrying. Norman, his name is.'

# 8

'Who are you, exactly?'

Mrs Dauncy perched on the edge of a balloon-backed chair and stared accusingly at Newton. A heavy jet necklace weighed round her neck; under her black bonnet, her hair was raked into a bun. A corseted mourning gown sculpted her plump figure. She sat poker-backed with her hands clasped in her lap, the only position she found even slightly comfortable; the severe expression on her round face made her look bad-tempered. As they were the only mourners, the Reverend Dauncy instructed his wife to take Newton and Abigail back to the vicarage.

The drawing room was crowded with examples of taxidermy: a vixen and her cubs nestled together on the mantelpiece; side tables supported glass domes with displays of hedgerow birds and their nests; a badger in a glass case was mounted over the door. An upright piano was tucked away in a far corner of the room and, for the sake of economy, there was no fire in the grate.

'No one is present at these types of funerals as a rule,' Mrs Dauncy said. 'That is why I make a point of attending; otherwise it would only be Dauncy and the gravedigger. I see it as one of the duties of a vicar's wife.'

'That's very good of you.' Abigail smiled.

'If Dauncy had warned me that you were coming, I should have asked the maid to prepare refreshments.'

'Just a cup of tea would be wonderful,' Abigail assured her.

'Tell me, what is your connection with the deceased woman?'

'Miss March saved her from drowning,' Newton interrupted.

'That was you?' Mrs Dauncy stared at Abigail. 'And you're not English.'

'Canadian,' Abigail said. 'I am visiting the country with my father. Unfortunately, he succumbed to bronchitis on the voyage; I am left to deputize for him. Mr Newton and his sergeant are escorting me.'

'You have your duties and I have mine, Miss March,' Mrs Dauncy said. 'I heard about what happened on the quay; I think the whole town is talking about it. No English-woman would have done what you did.'

The door opened and the Reverend Charles Dauncy stepped lightly in. He was thin, round-shouldered and leaned forward eagerly.

'Sorry, sorry, sorry.' He fluttered his hands each side of his head as though he was batting away a cloud of mosquitoes.

Dauncy directed a wide, tight-lipped smile at each of them in turn.

'Gravediggers,' he explained. 'Always arguing about money.'

Newton introduced himself and Abigail.

'The lady who threw herself into the river.' Dauncy beamed. 'My goodness.'

'Instinct,' Abigail said, unwilling to take any praise. 'I didn't think about what I was doing.'

'Nonsense.' Dauncy gave a little excited skip; for a split second, both his feet left the floor. 'Instinct is something possessed by the beasts of the field since they do not enjoy cognitive ability as we do. I believe you made a decision to jump, my dear.'

'I must have made it so quickly I didn't notice.' Abigail laughed.

'Aha.' Dauncy's eyes widened. 'Could this be because of your gender?'

He turned to Newton.

'I am sure the inspector or I would have been aware of what we were doing, had we decided to jump into the river.'

'Dauncy,' Mrs Dauncy hissed. 'Miss March has come to do her duty at a funeral.'

'This subject harks back to a conversation we have had many times, my dear.' Undeterred, Dauncy beamed brightly.

'Dauncy,' Mrs Dauncy said firmly. 'Do not continue.'

'The lightness of the female brain.' Dauncy took Newton by the sleeve and spoke in a gleeful whisper.

'Dauncy.' Mrs Dauncy's face glowed. 'I have requested that you do not continue.'

Dauncy gave one of his little excited skips.

'In my studies of anatomy,' Abigail said firmly, 'I have observed that the size of the brain is determined by the size of the skull which contains it. I think we can agree on that.'

'And, in general, the female skull is smaller than the male, is it not?' Dauncy beamed. 'A postiori, I rest my case.'

'And where is the evidence which suggests that the size of the brain dictates the power of its thoughts?' Abigail refused to let the matter lie.

'*Condemnant quod non intellegunt*,' said Dauncy lightly. 'They condemn who do not understand. I am not a scientist, Miss March, I merely take an interest in the scientific findings of others.' He glanced uncomfortably at his wife.

'Miss March and the inspector have come to pay their respects,' Mrs Dauncy hissed. 'They deserve seemly conversation, not to be entertained with scientific theories.'

'*Mea culpa, me paenitet*, my dear.' His feet planted firmly on the floor, Dauncy stared at the carpet.

'I notice that Superintendent Rawle is not represented.' Mrs Dauncy glared at her husband. 'I hope you will point this out to him. I hope you will also point out that it is a superintendent's job to clear women of this sort off the quay. If the wretch had been secure in the workhouse, she would be alive now.'

'My dear.' Dauncy tried to pacify her. 'I know you feel strongly.'

'It is not right.' Mrs Dauncy was adamant. 'I insist you make this known to the superintendent.'

'My wife and I are believers in the workhouse, a most worthwhile institution,' Dauncy said. 'I myself am a member of the Board of Guardians and Mrs Dauncy makes regular visits to provide the souls who reside there with edifying reading matter.'

'I arrange for Dauncy's sermons to be run off at the printers,' Mrs Dauncy explained. 'It is the least I can do.'

As the maid brought in a tray of tea, Dauncy brightened.

'I suggest you and I take our tea in my study.' Dauncy turned to Newton. 'While you are here, we should take the opportunity to discuss this other business.'

Abigail turned towards him.

'We shall leave you, ladies.' Dauncy gave one of his tight-lipped smiles. 'But not for long.'

As Newton followed Dauncy out into the tiled hall, he heard Mrs Dauncy apologize to Abigail for her husband's behaviour.

★　★　★

The station yard was empty when the carriage drew up. Still wearing a black armband on his sleeve, Newton climbed out first; Abigail followed him. A salt wind blew in from the estuary; above the town, clouds hurtled inland. Newton checked the sky for rain.

Attracted by the noise of the carriage wheels, Westcott appeared in the doorway. He studied them suspiciously, belly stuck out, thumbs in his waistcoat pockets.

'Exeter train ain't till this evening.' He sounded irritated. 'You've got your times wrong.'

'We're not here for a train,' Abigail said.

Her disarming smile failed to move Westcott; his ill-tempered stare followed her as she crossed the yard towards him. Newton told the carriage to wait.

'Is Norman here?'

'Norman?' Westcott considered. 'Why?'

'You may have heard, his brother has been sent to Exeter to stand trial at the assizes,' Newton interrupted briskly. 'Miss March is concerned for the boy's welfare.'

'Is she now?' Westcott stood with his legs planted apart watching them. He smelled of cider and looked as though he had slept in his clothes.

'Norman,' Westcott yelled.

A second later, Norman appeared from inside the building.

'What?'

He looked fed up even before he knew what Westcott wanted.

'This lady's worrying herself about you.'

'Why?' Norman squinted at Abigail.

'I'd like you to show me the station, Norman,' Abigail said pleasantly. 'You could take me for a walk up and down the platform.'

Norman looked at Westcott.

'If that's what the lady wants.' He caught Abigail's eye. 'I'm sure she'll make it worth your while.'

Norman shrugged and led Abigail through the station building and out on to the platform. Westcott turned sullenly to Newton.

'What's this sudden interest in the boy?'

'Miss March has an empathetic disposition,' Newton said. 'We heard what happened to his

136

brother. I take it someone has informed Norman.'

'Didn't have to.' Westcott shook his head; all this concern puzzled him. 'Two of Rawle's constables took him up the line first thing this morning. Norman waved him off.'

Newton cast his eye around the yard. A pile of packing cases stood by the doorway waiting to be moved on to the platform; a fringe of straw stuck up where the lids had been nailed down. Next to them half a dozen wooden crates were neatly stacked. A low trolley was loaded with parcels and mail sacks.

'The young lady needn't worry herself.' Westcott made an effort to be pleasant. 'We had the vicar up here first thing. Wants to send the boy to the workhouse. I told him, you might as well send him to gaol with his daft brother. Once you get inside that place, there ain't no getting out.' The station-master's face darkened. ''Course, he didn't take kindly to that.'

He swayed slightly, felt behind him for the door jamb and leaned against it.

'I told him, the boy's more useful here doing the fetching and carrying than he would be sitting on a bench picking oakum all day.'

'Miss March is concerned about the boy living on his own. We were informed he lived with his brother.'

Westcott snorted.

'Beds down on the mail sacks up here, most nights. It's his brother who was living on his own. I told the vicar to let him be; I'll make sure there's a shirt on his back so long as he does the fetching.'

'Miss March will be grateful,' Newton said.

A wagon drawn by two drays pulled into the yard. The stationmaster raised a hand to salute the driver.

'Last load, Westcott.' The driver jerked his thumb over his shoulder to indicate the pile of crates. 'Where's Norman? I can't unload this lot by myself.'

'Busy,' the stationmaster called. 'I'll send him along directly. You'll have to manage for now.'

He pulled Newton by the sleeve and headed through the station building. Abigail and Norman sat on a bench at the far end of the platform. She leaned close, anxious to catch everything he said.

'If we stay out there, he'll be on at me to fetch Norman to help with the unloading,' Westcott said. 'That means he sits there with his feet up while the boy does all the work.'

Leaving Norman where he was, Abigail got up and walked towards them up the platform. She beamed at Westcott.

'Now, Mr Westcott, I want you to let me

into the secret of your daffodils. I have never seen such a brilliant display; they are truly wonderful. Spring flowers are my favourite.'

Westcott blushed proudly.

'No one takes no notice of my daffs, as a rule,' he confessed.

'Perhaps you would show them to me, while the inspector has a word with Norman.' She smiled again. 'It will be a treat.'

Norman's face was pale and there were dark rings under his eyes; his clothes were pitifully thin, but as he was accustomed to the cold, the wind did not make him shiver. He watched Newton intently as he made his way up the platform.

'The lady wants me to tell you Edward never done it.' Norman stared at a crack between the flagstones under his feet. 'I told the superintendent. I told the vicar.'

'What makes you so sure?'

The boy looked up at Newton. 'Reverend Dauncy wants to take me off to the workhouse.'

'You would rather stay here?'

''Course I would,' Norman said sharply. 'I do the fetching and carrying.'

At the other end of the platform, Abigail was stooped over the bed of daffodils, smiling up at Westcott. Newton saw her disarm him. He stood upright and square-shouldered, unhitched his thumbs from his waistcoat pockets and shaped his hands to demonstrate how carefully he carried out the planting.

'Tell me, how you can be certain Edward didn't . . . ' Newton hesitated. Norman seemed so wretched it seemed cruel even to ask him.

'Cut her throat?' Norman looked at Newton.

What colour there was, drained from his face. His thin cheekbones looked cut out of chalk; shadows were scooped under his eyes.

'Edward was at home.'

'With you?' Newton said. 'You can swear to it?'

'Not with me,' Norman said. 'I left him there asleep. Mr Westcott lets me keep pieces of coal for my wages if they fall on the track. I made up a fire. Edward was asleep when I left and asleep when I got back.'

'What time was this?' Newton said. 'What night?'

'Monday; same day you arrived. It wasn't dark when I went out, but it was by the time I got home.'

Norman searched Newton's face, to find out whether he was being believed.

'And where did you go when you went out?'

'The quay. That's where I always go, unless I'm here.'

'What are you saying?' Newton struggled to

see what he was driving at.

Neither Superintendent Rawle nor the Reverend Dauncy believed the boy. Newton wondered if they had listened to him or whether they simply dismissed whatever he said as a loyal attempt to save his brother.

Far down the platform, both Abigail and the stationmaster were crouching down examining the bright trumpets of the daffodils. Snatches of their laughter carried on the breeze.

'I went guttering down on the quay,' Norman went on.

'Guttering?' Newton looked puzzled.

'Looking in the gutters for farthings people have dropped. You find pennies, sixpences, all sorts.' Norman looked at him suspiciously. 'You won't tell no one?'

Newton shook his head.

'Only Reverend Dauncy says it's taking what doesn't belong to you, which is stealing, so I didn't tell him about it. But the lady said I was to tell you every detail and you wouldn't mind.'

'I won't mention it,' Newton assured him.

'I got down to where that boat with the broken mast is. I hadn't found anything, only a comb. There were these men on the deck, two of them. They were holding a woman by one of her arms. She was kicking and screaming something terrible; she spat right

141

in the face of one of them. They'd pulled her out of the hold and wouldn't let go of her.'

'Do you know these men?' Newton said. 'Would you recognize them again?'

Norman shook his head violently and stared at the ground.

'What happened then?'

'She had a knife; she was pointing it at them, screaming her head off. They grabbed it off her and . . . '

'Go on,' Newton prompted.

'I ran off.'

Newton hesitated. 'One minute you watched all this going on and then you just ran off.'

'I was crouched in the shadows,' Norman said. 'Like I do so the Watch don't see me.'

'Why?'

'They chucked the knife aside. It landed right at my feet so I grabbed it.' Norman stared over Newton's shoulder down the station platform. 'They saw me.'

'You saw what happened while these men were holding the woman?' Newton had to be sure.

Norman nodded. He was barely listening; something caught his attention.

'Are you saying your brother took the knife off you?'

'I gave it to him; we share everything we pick up in the gutters. I came up here to sleep. He must have gone out to see if there was anything I missed . . . '

Suddenly Norman lost interest; he looked sick.

Red-faced and gesturing agitatedly, the Reverend Dauncy was arguing with Abigail outside the station house. Westcott joined in. The smile Abigail had brought to Westcott's face had gone; his belly pushed open the jacket of his uniform and his thumbs were back in his waistcoat pockets.

'He's come for me,' Norman muttered.

As he jumped to his feet, Newton grabbed his arm.

'Let me go.'

Trying to shake himself free, Norman swung wildly at Newton with his other hand. Tears of rage exploded behind his eyes.

'Wait.' Newton hung on tight. 'Miss March is standing up for you against the vicar. She's on your side.'

Norman stared. Down the platform, Westcott, red-faced now, pointed towards the station exit. Dauncy held his hands out in front of him as though he were handing over a glass globe. Abigail stood back for a moment and let both men attempt to face each other down. Then she stepped forward, lightly rested a hand on each of their arms and, each in turn, looked them in the eye.

Dauncy's arms dropped to his sides; Westcott took a pace backwards and tucked his thumbs in his waistcoat pockets.

'Patience,' Newton said.

Norman tried to wriggle free again; Newton kept his grip tight.

After a few minutes, Abigail beckoned; Westcott and the vicar stared up the platform as Newton led Norman towards them.

'The Reverend Dauncy has secured a parish place for Norman.' Abigail wore a diplomatic smile. 'And has gone to considerable trouble to do so.'

Norman squirmed; Newton tightened his grip.

'Mr Westcott has emphasized how important Norman's work is here.' Abigail turned to him. 'He provides coal for Norman to take home and Norman regularly receives gratuities from the passengers.'

Westcott glared at the vicar.

'We have all agreed that Norman will continue to work here every day under Mr Westcott's supervision until poor Edward's trial is over. Then the situation will be reviewed. In the meantime, I shall provide funds for a new jacket, breeches and shoes for Norman. I shall also let Mr Westcott have a small sum so that Norman may be sure of a hot meal every day.'

Westcott looked triumphant.

'This is a temporary measure,' Abigail said. 'Until the outcome of the trial is known.'

The spring had gone out of Dauncy's step.

'I have also offered that Norman takes his daily meal at the vicarage; my wife would be able to ensure that the boy is properly nourished.'

'He will eat here with me.' Westcott's belly pushed the flaps of his jacket aside. 'As he does do already and as he wishes to continue doing.'

'This is what we have agreed upon, Mr Westcott.' Abigail touched his arm again.

'As a temporary measure.' Dauncy wanted the last word.

Abigail turned to Norman.

'Have you got anything to say, Norman?'

'Thank you, miss.' Norman said. 'When will Edward's trial be over?'

Newton walked the vicar through the station building to where his horse was tethered in the yard.

'I had no idea you and Miss March took an interest in town urchins,' Dauncy said. 'Most laudable. I must say, Miss March argues cogently for someone of her sex.'

As Dauncy turned in his saddle to wave a cheery goodbye from the entrance to the station yard, Abigail joined Newton.

'Superintendent Rawle expects us to leave by the next train,' Newton said. 'He believes the investigation is closed.'

'How convenient.' Abigail looked at him. 'We must defend the defenceless, Inspector. Norman has no one to care for him; he tells me he has looked after his elder brother since their parents died. Now the Reverend Dauncy is threatening to lock him away in the workhouse.'

'I believe he is witness to the murder on the quay,' Newton said. 'Rawle will not take my word unless I am able to provide him with proof.'

'Then I will help you to find it,' Abigail said. 'Norman and his brother are little more than children; one is threatened with the gallows and the other with the workhouse. To condemn an innocent child to the workhouse merely because he is alone in the world is a most heinous cruelty.'

The fierceness of her conviction brought fire to her cheek.

'If I may, I should like to enquire about the other business that Dauncy deemed unseemly for the ears of females. Has it got anything to do with these children?'

'Nothing,' Newton said quickly. He knew Abigail noticed the colour in his face and heard the suddenness in his voice. 'It was something else entirely.'

Just as the carter unloaded the last crate and climbed back up into his seat, Norman sauntered out of the station building.

'Where have you been hiding, you little blighter? You left me with this lot.'

The man was short of breath.

'The vicar wanted to send me to the workhouse, but the kind lady says I don't have to go,' Norman said.

'Workhouse is too good for you, if you ask me,' the carter grumbled. 'I'm not so young as I was. Lucky I didn't do my back, shifting this lot on my own.'

'What's in these boxes?' Newton interrupted.

'Packing cases are from the pottery.' The carter looked surprised. 'Crates are from the collar factory. And that's the mail.'

Newton inspected the packing cases; a destination address in Exeter was painted on the sides. The wooden crates were headed for wholesale warehouses in London, Manchester and Liverpool. On the sides were stencilled the words 'Marathon reversible collars, cuffs, fronts, ladies' sets.'

'The lady says she's going to buy me a jacket and breeches and a new pair of boots,' Norman announced proudly.

Colour returned to his face. It was the first time Newton has seen him smile.

# 9

The skipper leapt off the boat on to the quay and faced Newton and Culley. He was about thirty, strong, and agile. Salt matted his straw-coloured hair and his face was bronzed by the wind. He and the men were stowing the gear when Culley called him over.

'This is the inspector I told you about,' Culley said.

The man grasped Newton's hand and smiled at him.

'William Yeo.'

'Making ready, Mr Yeo?' Newton said.

'Killing time and losing money,' Yeo said. 'We've been waiting for the weather all week. The waves are too steep for us to venture past the bar.'

He pointed to the men.

'The boys have got mouths to feed. As soon as the wind drops we'll be away.'

'I understand you towed in the *Brianna*.'

Yeo nodded.

'We were the only crew willing to row round the headland. Not that Rawle gave us any thanks for it. Freeing her wasn't easy; the breakers drove her a long way up the marsh.

After what happened to her mast, she was lucky not to capsize.'

'I want to ask you about the rifles,' Newton said.

'Five cases below decks. Superintendent Rawle had us unload her where she lay. That was what we did; carried the cases over the skern to the pebble ridge and loaded 'em on a farm wagon.'

Aboard the fishing boat, the men stopped work; grateful for a break, they hunkered down beside the line of lobster pots.

'There was no monkey business; nothing went missing,' Yeo added. 'Rawle had his beady eye on us the whole time.'

'So you left nothing on the boat?' Newton watched Yeo's face carefully.

'We never saw that girl, if that's what you're asking.' Yeo smiled. 'She must have tucked herself away up in the fo'c's'le.'

'Tell him about the fol-de-rols, William,' one of the crew called up to him.

The men laughed.

'It's nothing.' Yeo's grin widened. 'The only other thing on board was a chest full of clothes. Dresses. Scarves. Baubles. Women's things.'

His cheeks reddened.

'Women's things?' Newton said. 'Expensive?'

He struggled to understand.

'No. Cheap stuff: cotton dresses, glass beads.'

'So whose was it?'

'Must have belonged to the crew.' Yeo shrugged. 'Presents for their wives and sweethearts. They were so anxious to get ashore, they left it all behind.'

Newton looked puzzled.

'The superintendent let us have it. Presents for our wives and sweethearts now.'

Behind Yeo on deck, the crew laughed.

At the far end of the quay, on the bridge, the blue uniforms of two patrolling constables caught Newton's eye. They came to a halt and stared along the moorings. They called out to fishermen they knew; there was some bantering conversation, although Newton was too far away to catch what was said. Then they stared and one of them pointed. Dodging between the farm carts, they hurried along the bridge and turned down on to the quay. Newton realized they were headed in his direction.

'You're sure there was nothing else?' He turned back to Yeo.

'I've told you, the hold was empty.' Yeo shrugged. 'Just the rifles. It hardly seemed worth making the voyage. Maybe she was riding too high in the water when the storm came and that's why her mast broke.'

'What about the crew's possessions?' Newton pressed him.

'Must have snatched them up as they left. There was a barrel of biscuits and a water keg, that was all.'

At the far end of the quay, the constables pushed through the crowd.

'The rifles were old,' Yeo went on. 'I'm no expert but they looked well used. Enfields. Looked as though they'd been buried and dug up.'

'What about the skipper and the crew?'

'Long gone by the time we got there.' Yeo shrugged.

Newton heard the constables shout his name. He ignored them.

The constables burst through the crowd. One of them was Lamb; his companion was shorter and heavily built. Both of them fought to catch their breath.

'Inspector,' Lamb gasped. 'Superintendent Rawle requests that you desist asking questions and requests your presence at the police station.'

'I shall question whom I like,' Newton snapped. 'Be about your business, Constable.'

Newton turned his back on him and faced the skipper.

'And none of the crew has returned to the boat, to your knowledge? After you towed her back here?'

'Do not answer him, William,' Lamb said.

'It is the superintendent's orders that I prevent the inspector from asking more questions and bring him to the police station.'

Yeo stared at Constable Lamb and then at Newton.

'You can remind your superintendent that he promised to pay my men for towing in this vessel,' Yeo snapped. 'Letting them have a trunkload of baubles is no payment.'

'I don't know nothing about that,' Lamb said. 'All I know is — '

'It's all right,' Newton said. 'I've finished questioning.'

'No one has been back to the craft since she's been moored up.' Yeo made a point of ignoring Lamb and turned to Newton. 'At least not so far as we've seen.'

'I'm warning you, William Yeo . . . ' Lamb's face reddened.

'Warning me what?' Yeo stared at him. 'You're going to chuck me in the Torridge like you did that poor girl?'

Down on the boat, the crew catcalled. Red-faced, Lamb pretended not to hear.

'Inspector.' It was Abigail's cheerful sing-song.

She steered Norman towards them through the crowd.

'Just look at him.'

New cap, jacket, shirt and breeches;

Norman exploded with pride and embarrass-
ment. He stared at the cobbles beneath his
shiny boots.

'Just look at his lordship.' Yeo clapped him
on the shoulder.

The men on the boat called out in approval;
Norman couldn't lift his head to look them in
the eye, let alone speak.

Abigail beamed proudly.

'Norman is a fine young man,' she announced. 'It's high time he dressed like one.'

'Thank you, miss.' Norman stared up at
her adoringly.

Newton took Norman by the shoulder and
stood him on the edge of the quay in front of
the crew.

'Head up, Norman; look these gentlemen
in the eye.'

He called out to the men on the boat.

'Three cheers for Norman in his new suit.'

As the fisherman obliged, Norman's grin
split his face.

'I need a new jacket, miss,' one of the crew
called.

'I ain't never had a new pair of boots,'
shouted another.

'That's quite enough.' Abigail laughed.
'Norman has to get back to his work at the
railway station. Mr Westcott relies on him. I
just wanted the inspector to see him.'

With one last fond look at Abigail, Norman ran off along the quay. Newton turned to the constables.

'Sergeant Culley will follow you to the station to see what the superintendent wants while I accompany Miss March back to the Newfoundland Inn. You can tell the superintendent I shall call in on him later.'

'Sir . . . ' Lamb tried to object. 'Superintendent Rawle asked us to bring you . . . '

'You heard what I said, Constable.'

With Culley and the constables making their way up the quay, Newton thanked Yeo.

'I don't take notice of John Lamb whether he's wearing a constable's uniform or no.' He jumped back on to the boat. 'Nothing else you want to ask me?'

'Were there any Gypsies camped up there on the headland?'

'There ain't been Gypsies near here since the autumn.' Yeo laughed. 'They arrive at fair time, then they're off again before winter sets in. Same every year.'

'I heard there was a camp on the headland,' Newton persisted.

'Only person out there was Jim Molland, the farmer,' Yeo said. 'He watched us put a line to the *Brianna*.'

Newton turned to go.

'When you see Superintendent Rawle, you

can remind him he promised my men a day's pay.' Yeo's face clouded. 'We ain't seen a penny yet.'

As they walked along the quay, Abigail protested that there was no need for Newton to accompany her.

'What does the superintendent want?'

'He wants us to leave everything alone,' Newton said. 'He wants us to stop asking questions and go back to London.'

'I have to make a report to my father.' Abigail turned to him.

'And I to my chief inspector,' Newton said. 'We shall stay here until we have plumbed the depths of all this.'

Above them clouds scudded in from the south-west; there was rain in the air. Along the quay, people moved towards the shelter of the doorways; on the boats, the men climbed down below decks.

'I need to talk to that boy again,' Newton said. 'He saw something the night Catalin was killed. I have broached the subject with him once; it will be easier for him to be forthcoming with me a second time.'

'Norman is a witness?' Abigail said. The prospect shocked her. 'If he is reluctant to tell you all he knows, it is because he is afraid.' She looked Newton in the eye. 'And there is much in his life to frighten him: what may happen to his brother; the threat of the work-house; the fear of hunger and cold. Westcott is not unkind to him, but he is barely able to look after himself; he does not know how to care for the boy.'

'Norman must tell me what he knows,' Newton said stiffly.

'Let me come with you when you speak to him,' Abigail said. 'I have his confidence.'

Newton nodded.

'If it turns out that he is a witness,' Abigail's mind leapt ahead, 'what will be the consequences?'

Newton looked at her for a moment as if he did not quite understand.

'Norman will have told the truth,' he said. 'He will have nothing on his conscience.'

'He will have made enemies.' Abigail faced him. 'Who will protect him when word gets out?'

'If word gets out,' Newton said, 'it will not be because of me.'

Abigail let Newton hurry on a few paces ahead of her until he found himself embar-rassed that she was no longer walking by his side.

'I can ask Superintendent Rawle to keep an eye . . . ' Newton offered.

'Rawle?' Abigail caught up with him. 'What can he or his constables do? Anyway, how do you know they are not involved in some way? A constable threw Catalin into the river.'

'This kind of accusation ... ' Newton hesitated. Abigail was suggesting something he had not thought of; the prospect appalled him.

'Is outrageous, I know.' Abigail said. 'But it is only outrageous because you are a police inspector.'

Newton had the curious sensation that she had unlocked a door for him; yet, as he pushed it open, he was not able to see what was inside; the feeling disorientated him.

'I have to see the superintendent.' Newton struggled to organize his thoughts.

Neither of them noticed Culley hurrying towards them. His collar was turned up and his head was bowed against the wind.

'Rawle wouldn't speak to me.' Culley was out of breath. 'He says it has to be you.'

'He didn't give you any indication of what he wanted?'

'None,' Culley said. 'But if you want to keep on the right side of him, you ought to hurry along there. He tore into that constable because he came back without you.'

'I want to hear what you have to say about the farm,' Newton said. 'Rawle can wait.'

'What about the boy?' Culley said. 'Did you get anything from him?

Newton caught Abigail's eye.

'Let's get in out of the wind.'

Newton steered them through the door of the Newfoundland Inn. Apart from a group of men at a corner table who concentrated on their euchre game, the bar was empty. The warm air smelled of woodsmoke; logs crackled in the grate. Newton led them to a table in the bay window. Outside, the wind whined through the rigging; mooring ropes creaked as the vessels lifted on the incoming tide; hungry gulls wheeled and cried against the grey sky.

Culley planted his elbows on the table and leaned forward.

'Didn't get anything out of that farmer.' He looked at Newton. 'He went off into a rant about Gypsies. He says no one believes him and Superintendent Rawle ignores him. He's adamant travellers have been camping out in the woods and that some of his ewes are missing.'

Newton stared through the window. Passers-by pulled their coats tightly around themselves and leaned into the wind.

'I took a look round some of the barns,' Culley went on. 'Hay for his milk herd, the remains of winter silage, nothing unusual. The yards are ankle deep in mud, hoof prints and cart tracks everywhere; you can't tell who's been where.'

'What about men who work out there?' Abigail said. 'Did they talk about Gypsies?'

'There aren't any. Molland and his wife see to the sheep and do the milking between them.'

Culley leaned over the table and whispered urgently.

'The place is poor, sir. A wreck on the skern would suit Molland very well.'

'Did you ask him about the tar barrels?' Newton said.

'Gypsies,' Culley said. 'I got the same answer you did.'

'If he caused the wreck, why didn't he take the rifles?' Abigail sat back in her chair.

Lizzie Hookway appeared at the table.

'Miss March, gentlemen.' She beamed at Abigail. 'How do you feel, miss?'

'You see how Mrs Hookway looks after me?' Abigail turned to the others.

Colour rising in her face, Lizzie Hookway pretended to fiddle with her apron.

'You are kindness itself, Lizzie,' Abigail went on.

'One of your brandies would go down a treat, Mrs Hookway.' Newton looked at the others.

As Lizzie Hookway hurried away, Abigail stared at Newton.

'The rifles were the cargo.' She was insistent. 'Why didn't he help himself to them? He could have hidden them or buried them in his fields. No one would be any the wiser.'

'You think he's telling the truth?' Newton let her have her say. 'The skipper of the *Snowdrop* said there haven't been Gypsies here for months.'

'Maybe he wrecked the boat and when he found she was carrying guns, changed his mind,' Culley said. 'He didn't know what to do with them so he called in the constables.'

Through the window Newton spied Constable Lamb hurrying past in the direction of the *Snowdrop*; he was clearly searching for them.

'Looks like we've been sent for.' Newton nodded towards the window. 'I wish to interview the boy again. We shall slip out now. Sergeant, when the constable passes by perhaps you could keep him occupied.'

Exposed on the bridge, the wind was biting. From this vantage point, Newton was able to watch Lamb peering in doorways along the quay. He saw Culley emerge from the Newfoundland Inn and beckon the constable inside. Abigail placed a hand on her hat, held it in place and kept up with Newton's brisk stride.

As they set foot in the station yard,

Norman skipped out to meet them.

'Miss.' The boy beamed.

Abigail pulled him towards her and hugged him before he had a chance to object. 'I've lit the fire in the waiting room, ready for the passengers for the five o'clock.' Red-faced, Norman took a step back from her. 'Ain't you got no luggage, miss? I could carry it for you.'

'Where's Mr Westcott?' Newton said.

'Asleep in his hammock in the office. I'm to wake him when the first passengers arrive.'

'Good.' Newton looked pleased. 'We've come for a word with you, Norman.'

'It ain't the vicar, is it?' Norman's face hardened. 'If he wants to take me to the workhouse, I'll run away.'

'Nothing like that,' Newton assured him.

A window from the waiting room looked out on to the platform. At the far end, the packing cases Newton had inspected earlier were piled ready for the goods van. Norman's coal fire blazed in the iron grate; heavy, brown-painted benches stood on each side of the room; the floorboards were swept and the air smelled of dust. Grateful for the warmth of the fire, Abigail took a seat on one of the benches and gestured Norman to come and sit beside her.

'What a wonderful fire, Norman. This will keep the passengers snug.'

'Thank you, miss.' He pointed to a scuttle beside the grate. 'I picked the coal off the track this morning.'

'You remember the men I was talking to earlier on the quay, Norman.' Newton stood with his hands behind his back and looked down at him.

'The men on the *Snowdrop*,' Norman said. 'Why?'

'You remember you told me you saw two men on the deck of the *Brianna* with that young woman.'

Norman stared at the floor.

'Earlier,' Newton prompted, 'when we were sitting at the end of the platform.'

Abigail tried to take Norman's hand, but he pulled away from her.

'So?'

'Did you see any of those men again today?' Newton struggled to make his voice light.

'What do you mean 'today'?' Norman screwed up his face.

Newton noticed him glance towards the door.

'I simply mean, did you see any of those men amongst the ones I was talking to on the quay today, when Miss March brought you over to show off your new clothes?'

Norman shifted away from Abigail and

162

pressed the palms of his hands down on to the bench. He stared down at the floorboards.

'Norman?' Abigail said gently. 'The inspector is asking you a question. He is not going to hurt you.'

Norman glared at her.

'So what?' he snapped.

'What do you mean?' Newton said.

He took a pace forward so that he stood between Norman and the door.

'So what if I did?' Norman answered.

Norman started to tap his foot violently. The sound drummed on the waiting-room boards. Norman seemed oblivious. He stared first at Abigail then at Newton; if he had to take them both on, he would.

'You mean,' Newton wanted to be clear, 'those men on the quay were the same men you saw on the boat with the young woman that night.'

The toe of Norman's boot danced on the wooden floor. He lowered his head again and stared resolutely down.

'You've got nothing to fear.' Abigail gently broke the silence.

Norman wouldn't look up.

'There's no one here.' Newton tried to match Abigail's tone. 'Whatever you tell us, no one will know.'

Norman continued staring at the floor.

'Norman, please,' Abigail appealed to him.

'If I tell you, will you get Edward out of prison?' Norman glared at Newton.

'Norman, he's due to stand trial, if he's innocent . . . '

'Of course he's innocent,' Norman screamed. 'No one will believe him just because he's gone in the head. And no one will believe me.'

'I'm sure the judge . . . ' Newton stumbled. 'When he hears the evidence . . . '

'The judge won't believe him.'

Grief and anger twisted Norman's face; tears welled in his eyes.

'So what if I saw someone on the quay? What do you care about Edward?'

'The judge,' Newton persisted. 'I am sure . . . '

'They'll hang him,' Norman said. His voice choked in his throat. 'And you won't do anything to stop them.'

'Who did you see on the quay?' Newton came out with it.

Norman sprang off the bench, angled himself round Newton and dived for the door. Abigail tried to catch him, but he was too quick. Newton made a grab and caught him by the shoulder. In one quick movement, Norman slipped free from his new jacket, grabbed the handle, yanked the door open and skipped out on to the platform.

Newton turned to give chase, but it was too late. Halfway across the yard, Norman turned to face him.

'He'll know it's me if I tell you,' Norman shouted. 'He'll come after me and cut my throat.'

Then he sprinted across the yard and out on to the road, leaving Newton holding his jacket, staring after him.

# 10

The moment Newton pushed open the office door, Superintendent Rawle was on his feet. As usual his desk was in apple-pie order. The folder of daily memoranda was closed; a pair of manilla envelopes lay precisely in the centre of the blotter; his pens, inkwell, a paperknife, stick of sealing wax and dish of bands and clips were lined up with military precision. Rawle was waiting for him.

'You should not be here.' Rawle spat the words like bullets. 'I told you to leave after the funeral.'

'The investigation — ' Newton sprang to his own defence.

Rawle didn't give him time to finish. 'Your sergeant has made a nuisance of himself.'

Newton felt the muscles tighten in his jaw. He stared straight at Rawle and held on to his temper.

'A local farmer has made a complaint,' Rawle continued. 'He found Sergeant Culley poking about in one of his barns without so much as a by-your-leave. Your man was fortunate not to come away with a backside full of buckshot.' Rawle glared at him. 'I hardly need to remind you of what trespass is.'

'I spoke to Molland, myself.' Newton snapped. 'Sergeant Culley was pursuing a line of inquiry.'

'And what did he tell you?' Colour drained out of Rawle's face.

'That Gypsies have been stealing his sheep,' Newton said. 'When he reported this, the Borough Police ignored his request for assistance.'

'That is pure impertinence, Inspector.' Rawle's hands hurried over his desk and straightened every object in turn. 'I imagine he omitted to tell you about the complaint he made that someone was stealing his milk or that his wife is regularly short-changed when she brings her vegetables to market.' He looked up. 'The fellow makes some kind of complaint almost every week.'

Rawle studied the alignment of the envelopes on his blotter.

'When he came in to report that there had been a wreck, he is lucky we believed him at all. Not being a local man, you would be unaware of this.'

Rawle picked up the envelopes and tapped the edges together.

'However.' Rawle raised his head and glared at Newton. 'Trespass is trespass. I should be grateful if you would have a strong word with your sergeant.'

'Is that all?'

'No it is not,' Rawle snapped.

He tapped the edges of the envelopes on the desk.

'When I request you come to my office, Inspector, I expect you to come in person, not send your sergeant.'

Rawle did not raise his voice. Keeping his anger cold made veins stand out in the sides of his neck; his face flushed pink.

'I have received another telegram from Scotland Yard demanding to know why you have not yet returned. As I told you yesterday, Inspector, your business is done here.'

Rawle held out the two envelopes.

'These came for you. One is yours, the other is addressed to Sergeant Culley.'

Opening the telegrams in front of Rawle was out of the question. Newton slid the envelopes into his pocket.

'I also had a visit from the Reverend Dauncy.' Rawle had clearly not finished. 'He has made arrangements for the infant discovered in your hotel room to be cared for by a young woman at the workhouse. I understand she is nursing her own child and has agreed to take on the foundling.'

'Naturally, I am glad to hear when any abandoned child is taken care of,' Newton said carefully. 'But I made it clear to you that this infant has no connection to me.'

'Apparently, Miss March has seen fit to take one of the town urchins under her wing.' Rawle stared accusingly.

'Miss March is a most charitable woman,' Newton flared. This was too much. 'Whom she decides to look after is her own concern, not that of the police superintendent.'

'The boy's brother is a murderer,' Rawle went on casually. 'He is in a cell awaiting trial at the Exeter assizes and will certainly hang.'

'I understand that the evidence is circumstantial,' Newton snapped. 'The young man is mentally impaired.'

'My constable arrested him at the scene of the crime with the murder weapon on his person.' A patronizing smile spread across Rawle's thin lips. 'When he asked him if he had committed the murder, he confessed.'

Rawle briefly scanned the papers on his desk; everything seemed to be in order.

'The vicar believes Miss March is raising false hopes in the brother of the accused. He lives alone now that his brother is incarcerated and spends his days running errands at the railway station. The vicar is concerned for the boy's welfare. He wishes him to be cared for by the parish so that when his brother departs this world, he will not be alone.

Apparently, Miss March is raising hopes in the boy that he can make some kind of living working for that drunkard, Westcott.'

'Miss March is an intelligent, sympathetic woman,' Newton said. 'She has the boy's best interests at heart.'

'He should be in the workhouse,' Rawle snapped. 'What will happen to him when Miss March leaves? She browbeat the vicar into letting him stay on at the station until the trial is over. What then?'

'The trial is not over.' Out of loyalty to Abigail, Newton dug in his heels. 'There is nothing to be served in locking the boy away in the workhouse before he needs to be.'

'He won't have long to wait,' Rawle said. 'The spring assizes are in session now. The judge has been apprised of the defendant's circumstances and read the statements; in the light of a guilty plea, the clerk of the court has added his name to the list. A noose will be around Edward Rumsam's neck by the end of the week.'

On the stairs, Newton decided not to open his telegram until he was out of the building.

The pieces of the jigsaw which had begun to come together were now flung apart. Gillis might be crying out for an update, but Newton still had nothing to report. Abigail's version of events to her father would cover

170

incompetence (loss of the rifles), an unsolved murder (Catalin) and a possible miscarriage of justice (Edward Rumsam). Any message Mr March carried back to the Dominion parliament would be the wrong one. And now, Abigail was on a doomed mission to save Norman from the parish.

On top of this, Newton had deliberately withheld information that was material to the case from the superintendent. He could hardly believe he had done this; it set all his instincts as a policeman into revolt. Norman had practically told him that he was witness to Catalin's murder. Newton knew if he breathed a word, Rawle would have Constable Lamb drag Norman to the police station and flog him until he gave up a name. Something else troubled Newton. If he hadn't met Abigail, would he have kept his own counsel? Would he have cared about sparing some urchin boy a whipping? He knew the answer.

The wind off the river rattled the shutters and flapped the blinds of the shops in Bridge Street. Pulling his jacket tight around him with one hand, Newton felt for the telegram with the other. He stepped into a doorway and slit open the envelope. *Finding guns unimportant. Stop. Point made. Stop. Murder's not our concern. Stop. Return London immediately. Stop. Yare.*

What was this? Newton struggled to make sense of it. Then he checked the heading. The telegram was addressed to Culley. His stomach lurched. Finding guns unimportant? Murder's not our concern? His mind raced back to his briefing at the Samson Club. *A most loyal and trustworthy man . . . carried out undercover work against Fenian cells in the past.*

Newton slid the telegram back into his pocket and then slit open the second envelope. It was addressed to him from Gillis. *Understand local difficulties. Stop. Satisfactory result essential. Stop. G.*

If he had thought about it, he might have expected Culley to be in contact with Sir Lawrence. But, *finding guns unimportant?* How could this be? He would have understood if the telegram read *best left to the local constables* or *not a matter for the Metropolitan branch*, but it didn't. A shipment of Fenian guns was washed up on England's shore and a Member of Parliament wanted it ignored? Something didn't make sense. He hurried back to the quay to find Culley.

Apart from Abigail, who occupied the seat closest to the fire, the Newfoundland Inn was empty. Lizzie Hookway had turfed out her customers and was attacking the flagstone floor with a mop and pail. Red-faced, she

172

grunted with the effort. She looked up sharply when Newton pushed open the door; if Abigail hadn't been there she wouldn't have let him in.

'I'm getting too old for this,' Lizzie grumbled. 'I need a youngster to help me. Trouble is nowadays they're all afraid of hard work.'

She dragged her bucket across the flagstones to the other side of the bar.

'A fisherman from the *Snowdrop* came for you,' Abigail said. 'He said the skipper has something to tell you. Sergeant Culley went in your place.'

'Did he say what it was?'

'No. But before you chase after him, Inspector, I also have something to say to you.' Abigail caught him by the sleeve.

Newton sat down opposite her.

'The young man, Edward Rumsam,' Abigail began. 'I am determined to speak with him and if he is innocent, I mean to do all I can to see that he is released.' She held up her hand. 'And before you try to talk me out of it, my mind is made up.'

'Rumsam has confessed to murder,' Newton said quietly. 'He was caught with the weapon on him.'

'What nonsense,' Abigail flared. 'I understand he could hardly tell you if it was day or night; even his brother will confirm that.'

'I have just come from the superintendent . . . ' Newton began.

'I will not stand by and do nothing. Norman is right: the young man has no one to speak for him.' Abigail locked her fingers together in front of her. 'He may have been coerced into making a confession. Has anyone thought of that? If he is found guilty, he will hang and Norman will be condemned to the workhouse.'

'The Reverend Dauncy — ' Newton began.

'The Reverend Dauncy will put him there,' Abigail snapped. 'And I am not surprised, being as he clearly has more understanding of dead animals than he has of live human beings.'

'He is concerned for Norman's welfare,' Newton insisted.

'He wishes to file him away like a sheet of paper,' Abigail said. 'He wishes to hand him over to the parish authorities and forget about him. I am determined, Inspector. I leave for Exeter on the morning train.'

'Miss March.' Newton floundered. He spoke slowly and deliberately. 'I am duty bound to escort you and I am not able to leave for Exeter tomorrow. You know matters here stand unresolved.'

'I know that if someone does not speak up for that young man, he will hang.' Abigail's voice shook. For the first time, her shield of perfect manners and generous humour slipped; Newton glimpsed the blazing anger which made her resolute.

'I do not require you to accompany me, Inspector. I am quite capable of sitting in a railway carriage by myself.'

'I only meant . . . ' Suddenly, Newton felt he wanted to apologize to her but some confusion in his brain meant he couldn't tell what he wanted to apologize for.

'I know what you meant, Inspector,' Abigail assured him. She smiled kindly. 'I know you do not have the time to accompany me, therefore I shall go alone. My mind is made up.'

Newton had it on the tip of his tongue to suggest Culley went with her. Then he remembered the telegram. *Murder's not our concern.* What did that mean?

'I cannot allow it.'

The words burst out of Newton before he had time to think. Abigail stared at him.

'I'm afraid, Inspector, you have no choice.' Abigail's smile was fixed in place.

In the corner of the parlour, Lizzie Hookway put down her mop.

'I'll come with you, miss.' Hardly believing her own temerity, she fiddled with her apron. 'I haven't been to Exeter since last summer.

I'd love a ride on the train. That's if the Inspector thinks . . . '

Newton stared at her.

'I think that is the most wonderful idea . . . ' Abigail interrupted.

'I wasn't eavesdropping, miss.' Lizzie Hookway was suddenly flustered. 'Only, I couldn't help overhearing. I could leave this place in the hands of the barman for a day.'

'That would be grand,' Abigail said. 'You could act as my guide. I expect you know where the lawyers' chambers are.'

'In the cathedral close, miss, only a short cab ride from the station.'

'There.' Abigail beamed at Newton. 'You see how Lizzie looks after me?'

'The morning train leaves at nine.' Lizzie Hookway couldn't contain herself. 'We will be able to return in the afternoon. I shall pack a hamper for the journey.'

'I shall arrange a meeting with the prosecuting counsel and then I shall ask you to take us to the teashop where we will find the best cakes in the city,' Abigail said.

Lizzie Hookway turned to Newton.

'You needn't worry, Inspector.' She glowed with the excitement of it. 'I shan't let any harm come to her.'

There was a cautious tap at the window; faces of the men waiting to be let in were pressed against it. With a curt flap of her hand, Lizzie Hookway indicated that she did not wish to be disturbed. She was anxious to consult Abigail on the topic of food for the journey. Newton noticed Culley in the crowd outside; he left Lizzie Hookway's excited discussion of sweet and savoury and headed for the door.

Outside, with a good view of the fire through the window, the crowd grumbled about the cold. Newton grabbed Culley by the arm and towed him up the quay.

'Yeo has something to tell you,' Culley began. 'You weren't here, so . . . '

'That cockalorum, Rawle, wanted to give me these in person.' Newton pulled the crumpled telegrams from his pocket. 'I opened yours by mistake.'

Culley smoothed out the paper and glanced at it.

'They want us back in London.' He shrugged.

'*Finding guns unimportant?*' Newton said. 'You're keeping something back from me, sergeant.'

'What might that be?' Culley glared at him. 'What are you talking about?'

'We were sent all the way down here so Miss March could see these rifles with her own eyes, as proof that the Fenian threat is being dealt with. Now, all of a sudden it seems this doesn't matter.'

'What do you want me to say?' Culley's face hardened. 'I'm a police sergeant, not a politician.'

'And how did Sir Lawrence know the rifles were missing?' Newton continued. 'I didn't tell him.'

'He appointed me,' Culley said. 'He wants to know what's going on.'

'I am in charge.' Newton glared at him. 'Communication with London goes through me.'

'I worked for Sir Lawrence in Ireland.' Culley tried to explain.

'We're not in Ireland now. You are my sergeant.'

Culley walked a few paces ahead and stared out across the river. Pillows of dirty cloud blocked the sky; gulls screamed. On the rising tide, boats heaved at their moorings.

'Sir Lawrence requires me to report to him,' Culley said. 'That's all there is to it. And now he wants us back in London, we'd better go. There's a train this evening.'

'We won't be on it,' Newton said. 'There is police work to do here. I will not leave until the rifles are found. Besides that, Miss March is going to Exeter tomorrow to plead the case of the young man who is accused of killing the girl.'

'Rumsam?' Culley looked amazed. 'The lunatic?'

'He has no one to speak up for him,' Newton said quietly. 'Miss March has decided it is her duty to do so.'

'And you agree with this?' Culley made no attempt to hide the sneer in his voice. 'A constable found the fellow with the knife in his belt staring at the vessel where the girl's body was found. What does Miss March think she is going to do, persuade the judge that it was in the constable's imagination?'

'She believes Rumsam does not know what he is saying,' Newton said. 'She believes he is suggestible. Someone could have told him what he is supposed to have done and he believed them.'

'I heard the same from the skipper of the *Snowdrop*. But would you expect anything different? He's no friend of Rawle and his constables, is he?' Culley laughed. Then he noticed something in Newton's manner. 'For God's sake, are you telling me you go along with this?'

In that moment, Newton knew.

'Yes, I am,' he said. 'The course Miss March has chosen is the right one.'

Further along the quay, the *Snowdrop* strained at her moorings. The decks were scrubbed, the lobster pots lined up, the nets repaired and squared away. As soon as he noticed Newton, Yeo leapt the gap between the gunwale and the quay.

'Just tell the inspector what you told me.' Culley sounded resigned.

'I heard that Edward Rumsam has confessed,' Yeo said. 'Sounds to me like a piece of nonsense dreamed up by Rawle's constables. Edward wouldn't hurt a fly. Day in, day out he sits on the quay staring up at the seagulls. Whenever someone needs a hand, he jumps to it like a soldier. The drivers get him to shovel up the horse dung; he'll run errands, anything.'

'You know him well?' Newton glanced at Culley.

'Everyone on the quay knows him. He's always down here, his brother too. The men find him jobs when they've got a few farthings to spare; someone will always slip him a piece of fish when the catch comes in.' Yeo laughed. 'Some days he has a better supper than me.'

'Thank you,' Newton said.

'Which one of them arrested him?'

'Constable Lamb, I believe.'

'I've told you before,' Yeo said. 'John Lamb should not be allowed a uniform.'

'You're familiar with him?' Newton closed in; this was what he had expected.

'Known him since he was a boy.' Yeo laughed bitterly. 'His father had a cottage out on the skern. He worked the lime kiln Molland used to have out there. Then his wife ran off and the boys ran wild, John and his older brother. Old man Lamb was fond of the cider jug; when he was in drink, out came his belt and woe betide whoever was in reach.'

'Then he will have learned the consequences of his actions.' Culley appealed to Newton. 'You can't say a constable wrongly accuses someone of murder just because his father kept him in line when he was young.'

'Lamb and his brother were brought up harder than most,' Yeo said. 'Edward Rumsam wouldn't hurt a fly. That's all I'm saying.'

On the way back to the Newfoundland Inn, Newton tried to make the position clear to Culley.

'A shipment of smuggled guns disappears,' he said. 'A girl has her throat cut; the constables arrest someone who is simple-minded and harmless.'

'We should be making our way back to London,' Culley insisted. 'The conduct of incompetent borough constables is not our concern.'

The Newfoundland Inn was crammed. Euchre players took over the tables and drinkers crowded the bar. The air was the usual warm cushion of pipe tobacco, woodsmoke and the aroma of cider. Abigail was nowhere to be seen; a barman stood in Lizzie Hookway's usual place. He was on the lookout and he elbowed his way through as he spotted them.

'Inspector Newton, ain't it? Miss March says to tell you she had to go to the vicarage.'

Newton must have looked concerned.

'Don't you worry, sir,' the barman assured him. 'Mrs Dauncy sent the maid down in a carriage to collect her. She said to come at once. It was something of the utmost importance.'

'She's there now?' Newton said.

'Yes, sir. She left half an hour ago.'

'Did the maid ask for me?'

'No sir. The request was for Miss March alone.'

# 11

At the vicarage, a chink of light showed through the drawing-room curtains and a lamp had been lit in an upstairs room. As Newton climbed down from the carriage, the front door opened and a young woman picked her way down the stone steps. Dressed in a serving girl's bonnet and shawl, she glanced briefly up at him as she hurried past into the shadows. In the light of the carriage lantern, he caught a glimpse of her tear-stained face.

Dauncy stood at the door and peered after her. He was in a state of high agitation.

'Another visitor. Inspector. My goodness.' He hopped from one foot to the other. 'News travels fast. Or have you come to enquire about the baby?'

'I have not. I merely . . . '

'Come in, come in.' Dauncy pulled the door wide.

The hallway was in darkness. Yellow light drew a line round the edge of the drawing-room door. Instead of opening it as Newton expected, Dauncy fumbled with a match and lit the oil lamp on the hall table. Immediately, the stuffed head of a roe deer reared at them out of the shadows.

'I've been banished.' Dauncy's voice dropped to a whisper. 'We should go to my study.'

Newton followed the vicar up the stairs. The walls were lined with books; the oak desk in front of the window faced into the room. The air was stale and warm from the coals which glowed in the iron grate; studded leather chairs stood on each side of the fire. The room was lit by oil lamps, one on each end of the high mantelpiece. Dauncy carefully left the door ajar.

'They've got the maid in there.' He spoke quickly in a whisper. 'That's why I had to answer the door. Now, the baby. There is no need for you to concern yourself. The Board of Guardians will formalize the situation at their meeting this evening. A suitable young woman has been identified and the infant has been placed in her care. She already resides in the workhouse and has a child herself so a second will give her no trouble. The overseer will put her on light duties until both infants are weaned.'

'I understand Miss March has called on Mrs Dauncy,' Newton began. 'I am required to accompany her . . . '

Dauncy gestured him to sit and took the opposite chair.

'Then you have not come to enquire after the baby?' He looked confused. 'There have been so many comings and goings this evening. First the foreign girl, then my wife summoned Miss March, then poor Charlotte was on the doorstep with her tale of woe. Then you arrived, Inspector.'

'Naturally, I am pleased the child is suitably looked after.' Newton had to spell it out for him. 'But I am here to see Miss March.'

'No, no, no. I am not allowed in there, nor will you be.' Dauncy's fingers fluttered nervously each side of his face. 'Best leave them to it. My wife felt, under the circumstances, a male presence . . . '

His words drifted away.

'I'm sorry?' Newton had no idea what the man was talking about.

Dauncy leaned forward confidentially.

'I found her collapsed on the floor of the nave. At first, I thought she was dead.'

Dauncy's agitated fingers played a piano scale on his knees.

'I didn't know what to do.' He appealed to Newton. 'Whether to call the constable . . . ' His words drifted again. 'They've got the maid in there. I suppose they're feeding her and finding clothes for her.' Dauncy stared at him. 'I thought she was dead, you see . . . '

Newton's heart crashed in his chest. For a terrible moment, he thought Dauncy was talking about Abigail.

'Who do you mean?'

Dauncy looked blank.

'That's just it.'

His fingers played a minor chord. He stared earnestly at Newton. In the lamplight, his eyes were wide with worry.

'I got her to her feet and had to half-carry her back here. The poor wretch only had on a thin dress, no coat, no shoes. Just now, I heard the maid heating kettles for a bath. I expect that's what they're doing. A hot bath. She will have brought the bath down in front of the fire.'

'Who are you talking about?' Newton pressed him.

'My wife sent for Miss March.' Dauncy drummed his fingers on his knees. 'Because of the language. Neither of us could understand a word.'

'French?' Newton's mind raced.

'I don't know.' Dauncy's fingers wriggled. 'She has an accent; it could be Spanish. I have no idea.' Dauncy was wretched. 'If only the maid . . . I could order some tea . . . '

At the sound of movement in the hallway downstairs, he jumped up.

'Anyway, I have to leave.' He pulled out a

fob watch from his waistcoat. 'I have a meeting with the Board of Guardians. Inspector . . . ' He appealed to Newton. 'Please wait here. Settle yourself by the fire. I'm sure that by the time I get back . . . '

Before Newton could get up, Dauncy slid backwards out of the door. His footsteps clattered on the wooden stairs. Newton heard voices in the hall followed by the slam of the front door.

Newton followed the vicar downstairs.

'Inspector.' In the hallway, Mrs Dauncy's petticoats swished. 'I was unaware Dauncy had a visitor.'

Abigail pulled the parlour door closed after her. A smell of chicken broth lingered in the air.

'Please keep your voice down.' Abigail hushed him before he had a chance to open his mouth. 'I have settled her on the couch. She must rest.'

'The maid will light a fire in the spare bedroom and put warming pans in the bed,' Mrs Dauncy said. 'We will get her upstairs as soon as the chill is out of the air.'

'Did you follow me, Inspector?' Abigail said.

'At the Newfoundland Inn, they said you had gone to the vicarage, so . . . '

'That was very thoughtful of you.'

For a moment, it occurred to Newton that she was laughing at him.

'Naturally, I was concerned . . . ' His words stumbled.

'Thank you, Inspector.' Abigail smiled.

'What is going on?' Newton struggled to keep up. 'You have found another girl?'

'She speaks some dialect,' Abigail said. 'It isn't French; closer to Spanish perhaps. She is exhausted and weak. Mrs Dauncy has volunteered to care for her.'

'Dauncy found her prostrate in the nave.' Mrs Dauncy sounded horrified. 'He should have called a constable. What would have happened if she had died?'

'She's young; she won't die.' Abigail squeezed Mrs Dauncy's arm reassuringly. 'She needs rest and nourishment. I can't imagine when she last had a good meal.'

'Is she from the boat, the same as Catalin?'

Abigail hushed him again. Newton blushed, unaware that he had raised his voice.

'We must not wake her,' Abigail whispered. 'Where else would she be from?'

'I should be obliged if you would contact Superintendent Rawle for me, Inspector,' Mrs Dauncy said. 'If the girl is to stay here, I should feel better if there was a constable stationed outside the house.'

'I can do better,' Newton said. 'I shall send

my sergeant. He will come right away. There will be no need for you to trouble the superintendent tonight.'

'But I thought the constable on night watch might help us,' Mrs Dauncy said.

'My sergeant will come.' Newton was adamant.

Abigail caught his eye.

'I have to go to Exeter in the morning.' Abigail turned to Mrs Dauncy. 'But I shall call round early, on my way to the station.' She beamed. 'I am sure you will find there is no need for any potions or liniments. Warmth, rest and food are the best cure-alls. Besides that, I know I am leaving her in most capable hands. You are kindness itself, Mrs Dauncy.'

'Oh, well.' Mrs Dauncy briefly inspected the tiled floor. 'I shall do my best. Be assured, Miss March.'

Newton pointed out muddy patches in the vicarage drive and held the carriage door for Abigail. It was dark now; wind disturbed the high branches of the trees.

'There was really no need for you to follow me, Inspector.'

Newton couldn't see her face.

'The barman . . . ' Newton began to explain.

'I understand,' Abigail interrupted crisply. 'But there was no need for you to follow me.'

The carriage jolted over the stony road.

Although her words were clear enough, Newton was unable to grasp what she meant.

'Mrs Dauncy summoned me.' Abigail tried to help him. 'She thought I would be able to make out what the girl was saying. Besides that, she asked me for medical advice.'

'I am entrusted by your father, Miss March . . . ' Newton began.

'I do understand.' In the darkness, Newton knew she was smiling at him. 'But I do not wish you to cling to me like a shadow.'

Newton listened to the rattle of the wheels and the clop of the horses' hoofs. The carriage lurched. Through the small window, moonlight fringed the clouds, but the sky was black.

'Tell me about the girl,' he said.

'Starving, exhausted, frightened; what do you want to know about her?'

'You're sure she came from the *Brianna?*'

'Where else would she be from?' Abigail paused. 'I had to press Mrs Dauncy to let her stay. She was concerned that a girl from the quay should be there.' Abigail sounded suddenly dispirited. 'She said the vicarage was not the place; that the parishioners would gossip and she had to consider her husband's standing. Eventually she agreed that the girl could stay while she was nursed back to health.'

'And were you able to converse with the girl?'

'I have told you I couldn't understand her, Inspector. She was distraught; she wasn't French. I don't think she was speaking Spanish. She will be rested by the time I return from Exeter; I shall try again then.'

★   ★   ★

During the night, the wind rose again in the west and a storm lashed the roofs of the town. Rain beat hard along the quay. On the rising tide, the boats heaved against their ropes; in the wind, their rigging bent like wire. Anything that was not anchored down bowled the length of the quay: newspaper, sticks, straw from farm carts, all the detritus of the previous day lodged in gutters and doorways. The wind screamed past the moorings and moaned between the high buildings in Bridge Street; it was punctuated by the crash of roof slates exploding as they crashed onto the cobbles, pieces of masonry torn from under the eaves and the clang of metal bins being hurled down the narrow drangways. The door of the Newfoundland Inn was locked and bolted; there were no lights along the quay; everyone was indoors. Unable to keep a flame in their lanterns, the constables on night watch took shelter in shop doorways up the High Street; when the storm surged, they retreated to the police station to dry their uniform jackets in front of a fire.

★ ★ ★

After Abigail's visit to the vicarage in the morning, Newton insisted on escorting her and Lizzie Hookway to the station. Abigail avoided conversation and stared out of the carriage window as they crossed the bridge; she seemed to be conserving her strength. Lizzie Hookway was breathless with excitement; she sat with her best hat planted squarely on her head and a straw hamper the size of a suitcase on her lap. Trees were down all around, Westcott informed them. It was a miracle that the line from Torrington was clear. He stood on the platform with his thumbs in his waistcoat pockets and oversaw the embarkation of the passengers. The train was on time.

Norman ambushed Abigail and made a last attempt to persuade her to take him with her. She rehearsed her reasons once again. She was adamant, he was unlikely to be allowed into the lawyer's chambers. Anyway, introducing a child sibling of a defendant accused

192

of murder into the proceedings would be read by a hanging judge as a blatant attempt to sway judgement. She was not sure that Norman understood. And she concealed the real reason from him: if she was unsuccessful, she did not want Norman's last memory of his brother to be of him crying in a prison cell. Norman's pale face was solemn; Newton rested his hand on his shoulder. They watched the train pull out together.

'What's going to happen, mister?' Norman turned his face up to Newton.

'Miss March will do her best.' Newton squatted down so he could look Norman straight in the eye. 'I can promise you that.'

'But what if — '

'Have you got something to do today?' Newton interrupted him.

'Mr Westcott is sending me across to the collar factory. The crates ain't got the proper dockets so they can't be loaded.'

Norman pointed out a pile of long wooden boxes stacked at the end of the platform. Newton had seen them before with destinations such as Liverpool, Manchester and London scrawled on their sides.

'I'll keep you company,' Newton said.

From the bridge, they could see the deep channels the night tide had cut in the mud. Tree roots torn from the banks of the estuary were jammed against the arches of the bridge; trees were down on the open land at the far end of the quay. In dry dock at East-the-Water, caulkers inspected the hull of a skiff for storm damage; the yard echoed to the hammers and saws of the shipwrights. Up and down the quay, crewmen clambered over their boats to check the rigging.

Traffic on the bridge was held up by a flock of sheep. A shepherd marched on ahead, swinging his crook and touching his hat to the wagon drivers who pulled up to let him pass. Newton, Norman and the other pedestrians squeezed themselves against the parapet. Behind the flock, a tousle-haired dog kept his head low, scurried backwards and forwards, noticed everything and yapped at the stragglers.

'See those men over there.' Newton pointed out the crew of the *Snowdrop*.

Norman shook his head; he knew what was coming. He jammed his fists into his jacket pockets and hurried forward.

'We saw them the other day,' Newton said. 'They're the men who towed the *Brianna* in because of her broken mast.'

Norman stared at him.

'I know who they are.'

'You know what you told me.'

'What?'

'You told me you saw two of them on the deck of the boat with the girl.' Newton spoke casually, as if he was passing the time of day.

Norman peered in the direction of the quay.

'No I didn't.'

Newton took a breath and held on to his patience. He stared at the gulls which had settled on a mudbank in the middle of the river.

'Norman, I think — ' He intended to contradict the boy as gently as he could.

'It wasn't them,' Norman interrupted.

'Now, Norman . . . ' Careful, Newton thought, be careful or the boy will run off again.

'It wasn't,' Norman said again. He looked up at Newton. 'I said I saw one of 'em and I did. But it wasn't them. He wasn't on the deck, neither.'

'Someone else, then?' Newton said.

Norman nodded furiously and went back to staring at his feet.

'Someone keeping watch, perhaps?'

'I ain't saying no more,' Norman said.

Without looking back, Norman broke into a run. He jinxed round a farm cart, slid sideways through a group of pedestrians and was away, sidestepping through the crowd. He was gone. A minute later, Newton caught sight of him fifty yards ahead at the end of the bridge. Free of the crowd, he stormed across the quay, dodged the traffic and hurtled pell-mell up Bridge Street.

Should have left him to Abigail, Newton reprimanded himself, should have waited. He puzzled over Norman's answer. *Someone else.* Who did he mean? A hint like this meant Norman wanted to tell him, didn't it? The boy was plucking up courage, but for the moment, this was all he could manage.

Newton knew it would take time to get truthful answers to his questions. Norman was frightened, that was all. Somewhere, there was a key which would allow him to overcome his fear. If Newton couldn't find it, then Abigail would.

As Newton reached the end of the bridge, Culley shouldered his way through the morning crowd.

'A constable took over from me.' Culley glared at him. He looked washed out, exhausted. 'The vicar sent word to Rawle. He wanted a local man.'

'The girl?'

'Asleep,' Culley snapped. 'This is a waste of time.'

'You're suggesting we just abandon her?'

'It was your idea that we should stay here until the guns are found. Instead, I've been up all night babysitting a French tart.'

'We have to find a way of questioning her,' Newton said. 'You know that.'

'I know that we should be back in London. Those were Sir Lawrence's orders.'

Culley's abruptness bordered on impertinence. Once upon a time, Newton reflected, he would not have tolerated a sergeant addressing him in this way. Now, Newton put Culley's ill temper down to lack of sleep and shepherded him towards the Newfoundland Inn.

'We'll get some breakfast.'

'I'll tell you something else.' Culley would not be appeased. 'The story about the baby in your hotel room is going to be all over town today. The maid at the vicarage wouldn't shut up about it.'

Newton tried to ignore him.

'They know who the mother is. She came forward, says she wants the child back.'

Newton stopped and faced him.

'She came round to the vicarage and pleaded with Dauncy. The maid listened outside his study door and heard everything.'

'She wants the child back?' Newton couldn't work it out. 'Why did she leave it in my room?'

'She said her father made her do it. He said he was sick of having it in the house and if she didn't find a home for it, he was either going to drown it or take them both to the workhouse. Apparently her brother told her there was a gentleman from London staying at Tanton's.'

'Who is this girl?'

'One of the chambermaids, Charlotte Lamb.'

'Lamb? She's the constable's sister?'

Culley laughed.

'Lamb put her up to this?' Newton took a step backwards.

'Hardly going to admit to it, is he?' Culley was enjoying himself; payback for Newton making him stay up all night.

'The manager assured me his staff were above reproach. He went on about how he'd checked all their references himself.'

'She hasn't worked there long. She used to live up here, then she went back down to Cornwall to have the child. Now she's back.'

'As soon as she realized the child was going to end up in the workhouse, she changed her mind.' Newton found it hard to believe.

'It's going to be the talk of the town, sir.' Culley's tone was conciliatory.

'You're saying I should tell Miss March before she hears it from someone else?'

* * *

Once inside the Newfoundland Inn, Newton and Culley took the seat in the window and watched the crowd mill past. The barman brought them a plate of bread and cold cuts. Food brought colour to Culley's cheeks and took the edge off his temper.

'We've got no chance of finding the rifles.' He stared at Newton across the table. 'You know that, don't you?'

'Why is Sir Lawrence so keen on our heading back to London?' Newton had had enough of Culley's whingeing.

'They'll be buried,' Culley went on. 'That's why no one ever finds Fenian weapons. Probably only one or two people know the location.'

'They're here somewhere.' Newton was dogged.

'That's what they do at home . . . ' Culley stopped suddenly, as if he'd said too much.

'At home?' Newton picked it up.

'On the estate. They bury the guns in the fields. Nobody has a cat's chance of finding them.'

Culley switched his attention to the window.

'The estate?' Newton said.

'Where I was brought up.' Culley shrugged. 'My pa was one of Sir Lawrence's keepers.'

Pieces started to jigsaw together in Newton's brain.

'Your father was Sir Lawrence's game-keeper? I didn't even know Sir Lawrence had an estate in Ireland.'

'He was killed, my pa was.' Culley said. 'Chanced on a bunch of Fenians burying their guns one night. They shot him cold.'

His voice was dead; he sounded as if he was reading from a list.

'Sir Lawrence helped us,' Culley went on. 'Found my ma another cottage. Made sure I got an education.'

'Did he encourage you to join the police?' Newton began to understand.

'My pa had worked for him all his life, his father before him for Sir Lawrence's father. He was born on that estate, just like I was. Sir Lawrence made it his business to look after us.' Culley pushed his empty plate away from him and sat back in his chair. 'The Fenians hated him, of course. He was an English landlord who spent most of his time in London. Ireland for the Irish and all that.'

Newton nodded.

'Not many would have looked after a keeper's widow like he did,' Culley said fiercely. 'Got me a job with the Dublin police, made sure I wasn't overlooked when it came to promotion.'

'So why does he want us back in London so urgently?'

'His lordship's a politician.' Culley smiled. 'Who knows? If he says forget the guns, that's good enough for me. I told you, we're never going to find them anyway.'

'We cannot just abandon cases of weapons for any Tom, Dick or Harry to discover.' Newton looked at him hard. 'We are officers of the Metropolitan Police. This is English soil.'

'Take it from me,' Culley countered. 'They're buried. The boat was supposed to be headed for Liverpool until it was blown off course. It's possible the guns will be moved down the coast somewhere. One night a boat will collect them and no one will know.'

'Liverpool? How do you know?'

'It's the main port for Ireland, isn't it?' Culley said quickly.

'The storm blew itself out last night. The boats will sail on the evening tide,' Newton said. 'They'd be gone now if it was high water.' Thinking aloud, he nodded towards the window. 'Rawle reckons the guns are hidden out on the skern; he's probably right. Any one of these boats could drop anchor, load the guns and be away on the same tide.'

'You're saying we should ride out there and keep watch?' Culley felt vindicated.

'Any of them could sail up to Liverpool for a few days and not be missed,' Newton said.

'We should start by keeping an eye on the quay.' Culley got to his feet.

Having been moored up for a week, the vessels were in good shape. The decks were scrubbed, nets were repaired and everything was stowed away. The men found tasks to occupy themselves as all the work had been done. They were cheerful; the change in the weather lifted their spirits. Gulls wheeled and screamed high above them as if they too understood what the fine weather meant.

Newton and Culley picked their way over the mooring lines. They paused at the *Brianna*. Rigging was heaped on the deck, torn sails were piled anyhow, the broken mast was dumped on the mud beside her.

'I know that place,' Culley said. He pointed to the word Duncormac painted in faded letters along the stern. 'My ma and pa took me there when I was a boy. I don't remember why.'

'Holiday?' Newton was only half-listening. He was staring along the line of boats trying to decide which he would approach if he had a cargo of contraband to be delivered.

'We didn't have holidays.' Culley laughed at the thought of it. 'Don't think my pa knew what a holiday was. He was probably on some errand for his Sir Lawrence and got permission to take us along. Most likely he was taking a look at a young fellow who'd applied for an underkeeper's post, something like that.'

Newton concentrated on the boats. He couldn't make up his mind.

'Where is this place?' He was only half-interested.

'County Wexford, about fifty miles south from where we lived. None of us had ever seen the sea, that's why Pa took us.' Culley smiled to himself.

Newton turned to him abruptly; colour sank out of his face. He reeled from the explosion which had just gone off in his head; it took him a moment to recover.

'We're looking in the wrong place.'

'What?' Culley didn't follow.

Newton turned on his heel and started to march back along the quay. Culley hurried to keep up.

'I know where the guns are.'

# 12

Newton tore through the station building and out on to the empty platform. The crates were stacked at the far end ready for the goods van. The words Vincent and Duncan, Collars, Fronts and Cuffs were stencilled on each one. Later, someone had come along and scrawled the destinations in black ink.

'Open them.' Newton was breathless from his run across the bridge.

With nothing to jemmy the lids, Culley hurried back along the platform in the direction of the ticket office. Newton tested the weight of the topmost crate; it would take two men to lift it comfortably.

There was shouting from the station building. Culley hurried towards him with a claw hammer in his hand. Then Westcott emerged, red-faced and furious.

'Hey! What's your game?'

'I tried not to wake him up,' Culley called.

Westcott laboured up the platform until he came face to face with Newton.

'What's going on? He can't touch that.' Westcott looked as though he was about to burst. 'That's London and South Western property. Tell your sergeant.'

The nails screeched as Culley clawed them out of the wood. Westcott made a dive for Culley and tried to snatch the hammer; Newton shouldered him away.

'This is a criminal investigation. We have reason to believe those crates contain weapons.'

'They're from the collar factory,' Westcott bellowed. 'Have you gone mad?'

The lid came free. A line of cardboard boxes was tightly packed in straw. Culley looked at Newton.

'Open them.'

Culley broke the string and fumbled with the lid. Inside was a half-moon of cotton collars packed tightly around a ball of paper included to keep their shape.

'What did I tell you?' Westcott yelled.

He made another grab for the hammer. Culley backed away and held it out of reach.

'All of them,' Newton said. 'We have to be sure.'

He shoved Westcott's huge bulk away from the stack of crates.

'You're stark raving.' Westcott's eyes popped out of his head; his breath came in gasps. 'You think you can come down from London and start throwing your weight about? You think you're going to get away with this?'

He shook himself free of Newton, took a step back and tried to reclaim his dignity.

'Just make sure you put it all back together when you've finished.'

Culley levered lid after lid. The crates contained identical rows of boxes which in turn contained identical arcs of stiff collars. When Culley reached the last one and started to repair the damage, Westcott stood and glowered over him. He brushed aside Newton's apology.

'Too late for that. I'll be reporting this to Superintendent Rawle and the railway authorities. Soon as I get the paperwork, those crates will be on the next train.'

Culley handed over the claw hammer.

'Anyway.' Westcott glared accusingly at Newton. 'Where did that boy get to? Last time I saw him he was walking into town with you. That was hours ago.'

'We parted company on the bridge,' Newton said.

'Well, he should be back. A run up to the collar factory doesn't take all day.'

On their way back across the bridge, neither Newton nor Culley spoke. There was little activity along the quay. The vessels were ready to sail; the crews were waiting for the tide.

'I'll have to tell Rawle.' Newton broke the

silence. 'I was convinced those rifles were there and they'd been staring us in the face all along.'

He left Culley on the quay and headed to the police station.

★ ★ ★

'Why, in heaven's name, are you still here?' Rawle snapped.

Newton stood by the empty chairs in front of the desk. As he tried to explain, bad temper darkened Rawle's face like a bruise.

'If there is one single complaint from the manufacturers, I shall pass it directly to Scotland Yard.'

'My sergeant is asking questions on the quay.' Newton tried to put a patch on things.

'We have already searched the boats.' Rawle glared at him. 'My men spent hours questioning the skippers. What does your sergeant hope to gain?'

'He's good at talking to people,' Newton said. 'Sometimes you can pick up things if it's not an official interview.'

'I shall have men stationed out on the skern in time for the evening tide,' Rawle said. 'The rifles are sure to be hidden out there.'

Newton nodded.

'I have also got men searching the outlying

farms as we speak.'

Rawle picked up a paperknife and played it through his fingers, jutted his chin at Newton and looked down his nose.

'Have I forgotton anything, Inspector? Is there anything else Scotland Yard thinks I should do?'

Newton knew Rawle did not expect an answer, but decided to give one anyway.

'Local knowledge,' Newton said. 'A list of names must spring to mind, men who have been in trouble with the law in the past.'

Rawle replaced the knife, aligning it with the edge of the desk.

'Thank you, Inspector. That was the first thing I thought of.' A narrow smile touched the corners of his mouth. 'It appears the great Metropolitan branch is unable to help us provincial fellows after all.'

'We are all working towards the same end,' Newton said patiently.

'Precisely.' Rawle picked up the paperknife again. 'Then why didn't you bother to report the appearance of that girl last night? It was left to the Reverend Dauncy to notify us. He was most surprised to find out that I did not already know.'

Rawle did not wait for an answer.

'I understand Miss March was summoned to act as translator but in the event was unable to do so. I also understand Mrs Dauncy was prevailed upon against her will to allow a woman of that sort to stay in the vicarage. When she requested the presence of a constable, a local man whom she knew and felt she could trust, this was denied her. Instead, you assigned your Irish sergeant.'

'Culley is a good man,' Newton said.

'He may be.' Rawle lowered his voice almost to a whisper. 'He may not be. My point is that it is not what Mrs Dauncy requested.'

Rawle pushed his chair aside and stood up. He was sick of Newton, sick of Scotland Yard, sick of the lot of them.

'This morning I wired Chief Inspector Gillis. Once again, Inspector, I demand that you leave on the next train and take your sergeant and the Canadian woman with you. It is no longer simply a question of personal morality, no longer a question of the good name of the borough force being dragged down. You are actively hindering my investigation.'

'We shall not leave.' Newton said flatly. 'Make all the complaints you like. I have already made it clear, I was sent down here to oversee the inspection of the rifles. Thanks to the conduct of this station I have not yet been able to do this.' He had had enough of being ordered about. 'Besides, Miss March has gone to Exeter to plead for the Rumsam boy.'

Rawle froze.

'What?' The blood drained from his face.

'He has no one to speak for him,' Newton said. 'Miss March has taken it upon herself.'

'This is deliberate interference in a prosecution brought by the Borough Police. What are you playing at? Miss March is in your charge. Have you sent her down there?'

'I have not.' Newton tried to explain but Rawle wasn't listening.

'The boy signed a confession. He is a murderer.' Rawle was beside himself. 'I shall report this to your chief inspector. You will be thrown off the force for this.'

On the way down the stairs, Newton thought of Norman. If Abigail was not able to get him to spit out those names when she returned, he would have no choice but to hand him over to Rawle.

That evening, Abigail's train failed to arrive, no fire was lit in the waiting room and there was no sign of Norman — Newton paced the platform. A carriage which had driven over the bridge on the off chance of picking up fares didn't stay; the handful of people who had turned up to meet passengers checked the time and left. Westcott insisted he had received no word.

With darkness falling, Newton got up from the bench at the end of the platform. Westcott collared him as he passed the stationmaster's office. Propped against the doorway, his uniform was unbuttoned; he reeked of apples.

'If you see that boy, tell him to get himself back here right away.'

Through the open door, Newton could see coals glowing in the grate, Westcott's hammock slung across one corner of the room, and an untidy pile of old mail sacks in another. An empty cider jug lay on the floor beside a chair with the cushion split and horsehair bursting through.

'You can tell him I've got a rabbit for his supper and he can expect a thick ear for staying out all day.'

He looked accusingly at Newton.

'He left here with you this morning. I know he gets into games with other young wastrels down on the quay, but he's always back here by now.'

'Maybe he's gone home,' Newton said coldly.

'He'd have wanted to meet Miss March off the Exeter train, same as you, wouldn't he?'

The tide was rising fast as Newton crossed the bridge. In the dying light, the water was as black as engine oil. The current pushed upstream beneath the stone arches of the bridge, carelessly deposited estuary flotsam and carried with it the sharp smell of the sea. Along the quay, the boats were ready; within the hour the tide would be on the turn. The reflection of lantern light from the fishing smacks danced on the surface of the water and the shouts of the men carried across the quay. Candles stood in the windows of the houses; squares of lamplight lay like straw mats beneath the bay windows of the Newfoundland Inn.

If there was a derailment, Westcott would have heard, wouldn't he? Thoughts buzzed in Newton's head like flies — points failure, engine breakdown, anything could have happened.

As Newton stepped off the bridge, he looked for a carriage. The Dauncys were expecting Abigail; it would be better if he went in person to tell them. He spied Culley deep in conversation with the crew of the *Snowdrop*. They were laughing together, getting on well. Casting his eye along the quay, he noticed there were no constables about. Just as Rawle said, they must have left for the skern.

★   ★   ★

A maid opened the vicarage door. A moment later Mrs Dauncy's footsteps clicked along the tiled hall; her black silk dress rustled over her petticoats like leaves. Newton explained about the train.

'Miss March assured me she would return this evening.' Mrs Dauncy twisted her fingers together. 'We cannot understand a word the girl says. I have tried, the maid has tried, even Dauncy made an effort.'

As Newton suggested reasons why the train could have been delayed, Mrs Dauncy hardly listened.

'Since she woke up she has done nothing but eat. And the constable has been called away. While Dauncy is out on parish business, I am quite alone with this young woman. I had expected Superintendent Rawle to show more sympathy.'

Mrs Dauncy opened the door to the front parlour. Swaddled beneath several blankets, a girl was curled up in a chair by the fire. She was about nineteen years old, olive-skinned, with fine features, a narrow face and brown eyes. An empty plate and unused cutlery lay on the table beside her.

'Hello.' Newton smiled at her.

The girl drew her legs under her and pulled the blankets tight. Warily, she stared at him and then looked across at Mrs Dauncy for an explanation.

'You see.' Mrs Dauncy tutted. 'She can't even say hello.'

She leaned forward from the waist.

'The inspector is just saying hello, dear.'

The girl stared at her.

'Did she have anything with her when your husband found her?' Newton said.

'Nothing. The dress she wore was rags; she didn't even have any shoes. I understand that other girl who was found spoke French. This one doesn't seem to speak anything.'

Newton sat down opposite the girl. She watched him nervously and huddled down under the blankets.

'Inspector Newton.' He smiled again and pointed to his chest.

Then he pointed to her. The girl stared. Newton waited a moment before trying again.

'You see?' Mrs Dauncy interrupted.

'Catalin.' Newton looked straight at the girl. 'Do you know Catalin?'

'Catalin?' The girl's face lit up.

She chattered wildly. As she leaned forward in her chair the blanket slipped; Newton noticed a rope burn around her wrist. He sat back and shook his head. He exaggerated a shrug to show her he didn't understand.

'Catalin,' the girl repeated. 'Catalin.'

'She knows her,' Newton said.

'Who is this Catalin?' Mrs Dauncy was at the end of her tether.

'The other girl. The one Miss March spoke to.'

'Catalin.' The girl nodded at them.

'The poor wretch expects us to produce her,' Mrs Dauncy said. 'Doesn't she know?'

* * *

Newton ordered the carriage driver to take him to the railway station before dropping him at his hotel. He had to check, once more. As the wheels rattled over the cobbles, his thoughts went back to Gillis's telegram. *Satisfactory result essential.* Under the circumstances, Newton wondered what kind of result Gillis would consider satisfactory. And why was this *essential?* Gillis was under pressure. What wasn't he telling him?

Crossing the bridge, with the river high under the arches, Scotland Yard seemed a world away. The tide was on the turn. One by one, the boats slipped their moorings and let the current take them. Light from their masthead lanterns bounced on the surface of the water as they headed off like a line of jiggling glow worms past the quay, past the dry docks at East-the-Water, past the woods which ran down to the bend in the river, and continued silently out towards the estuary, the sand bar and the open sea.

There was a light in the stationmaster's office. Newton jumped down from the carriage and peered in at the window.

Westcott was slumped asleep in his hammock. Coals in the grate glowed red. The oil lamp on the table burned low. In the corner, the pile of mailbags where Norman slept was unoccupied.

★  ★  ★

Back in his hotel room, Newton lay fully clothed on the bed and stared at the ceiling. With Abigail not returned, how could he sleep? Again and again, he turned over in his mind what could have happened; the later it got, the more terrible his imaginings became. When he eventually drifted off to sleep, he dreamed of a railway cutting littered with bodies and carriages on their sides. He saw himself searching for Abigail amongst the carnage, unable to find her. He snapped awake, bathed in sweat.

Nothing did any good. He got up, strode up and down the room and lay down again. He lost track of time; he was in a part of the night where minutes stretched until they seemed like hours and yet when he checked his pocket watch, the hands had hardly moved. Fatigue wore at the edges of him. Harmless shadows looked sinister; the creak of a floorboard made his heart race. Unable to lie still, he got up and paced. The hotel was silent; when he pulled aside the curtains and peered out, the quay was pitch black.

Newton had just pulled his nightshirt over his head when a noise made him catch his breath, a little deliberate rasping sound. At first he took it to be a mouse nibbling the skirting. Then there was a movement outside, a footstep in the corridor. He held up the oil lamp which stood beside his bed. An envelope had been pushed under his door. His heart exploded in his chest.

The message was in black ink on thin paper in a plain, round hand. *The boy is safe. If you value his life, do not search for him.*

No signature. Newton wrenched open the door. The corridor was in blackness. He fought with his nightshirt, struggled to pull on his trousers and jammed his feet back into his boots; he felt the weight of the Webley in his jacket pocket. There was a sound in the street outside, the click of a door closing. The front door to the hotel? Newton dashed to the window. He caught the sound of hurrying footsteps. They didn't carry on along the quay as he expected; whoever it was turned up Bridge Street and climbed the hill into the heart of town.

Newton fumbled with his bootlaces; he grabbed his jacket and hurled himself out into the corridor, felt his way along the wall and down the stairs. Darkness bounced around him. He kept his left hand outstretched while his right slid down the banister; his boot heels echoed on the wooden treads. When he crossed the lobby and found the front door, it was unlocked. He slipped the Webley out of his pocket.

Outside, the night air knifed through Newton's clothes. The quay was inky-black. Clouds had blown in, cloaked the stars and hidden the moon. He hurried left up the hill and strained his ears to catch an echo of a footstep. There was no sound except the moan of the wind. But when he looked back, there was a light, the flicker of a lantern at the corner of the quay. One of the night watch was climbing the hill behind him.

'Constable.' Newton's shout rang out like a bell. 'Did you see anyone?'

There was a reply, but the wind snatched it. Leaving the constable to follow, Newton hurried blindly on into the darkness. He felt his way along a cottage wall with his left hand, still clutching the pistol in his right; his boots slipped on the cobbles; once or twice his ankle went over, wrenched by the uneven ground. He almost fell. By the time he reached the top of the hill, his lungs burned, the muscles of his calves had tightened: he had to stop.

The road widened here; ragged shadows hung in the hedges. Newton could feel the wind on his face. He looked back down the hill, but there was no light. Maybe the constable was not following; maybe he had gone for help. Maybe Newton had imagined the light. Had he heard a whistle? He waited for his breathing to steady; he had reached the edge of town.

Newton continued on, more slowly this time. He splashed though puddles; mud soaked his legs. As the wind pushed the clouds along, shapes of trees reared at him out of the darkness; he almost cannoned into a cart pulled up by the side of the road. He knew he was heading out towards the skern: the smell of the sea was in the air. Through the moving clouds, starlight allowed him to glimpse a lane bordered by towering hedges. He kept going. Sapling branches whipped his face; brambles caught his clothes; his boots slid in the mud. Ruts made by the wheels of farm carts made him stumble.

This far outside town, Newton didn't know whether to go on or turn back; he couldn't say for sure where he was. His legs ached; the cold was in his bones. He slowed to a walk. Why hadn't the constable caught him up? Whenever he stopped and listened, all he could hear was the charge of the wind through the trees and the bang of his heartbeat in his ears.

As Newton rounded a corner, the lane ran down to a crossroad. A candle lantern lit the shape of a farm cart lurched over to one side. Two men knelt in the road. Their angry voices snarled in the darkness, blaming each other. A wheel had come loose. Newton froze. He retreated into the shadows and watched as one backed against the cart and lifted it while the other man struggled to knock the wheel in place. A pin had sheered, one of them said; there was no telling how far they could make it without the wheel coming off again.

The more Newton eavesdropped, the more innocent the men seemed; most likely, a farmer and his son heading out to be at their fields by first light. One was definitely older and in charge. Maybe they could help him. After all, he heard running feet not cartwheels on the cobbles outside the hotel; he heard one man not two. They would know the twists and turns of the lanes and who lived where; they could tell him if anyone had passed.

Newton tucked the gun in his pocket, stepped out of the shadows and started down the lane. The men looked up at the sound of his boot heels on the stony ground. The man fitting the wheel picked up the lantern and held it out; he shouted something. Newton called out to them that he meant no harm.

'Have you seen anyone pass this way tonight?'

The men were silent.

'I was following someone,' Newton said. 'I wanted to know if anyone overtook you.'

He drew close. In the light from the lantern he saw one of the men was still supporting the cart; the wheel was not yet fixed.

'Let me hold the light for you,' Newton said.

The older man who was supporting the cart wore a jacket torn at the shoulder; his grey hair was unkempt. When the light shone in his eyes, he turned his face away. The young man was dark-haired; his face was thin and unshaven. When the old man grunted permission, he handed over the lantern and knelt in the mud to finish making good the alignment of the wheel. They lowered the cart between them and let the axle take the weight.

As he handed back the lantern, Newton noticed that the steel rims of the wheels were bound in rags, the sort used by undertakers to deaden the sound of a hearse. But these muffles were knotted and badly tied; over the lumpy roads, the uneven ride had caused the pin to sheer.

The faces of the men were in shadow. Newton thought they turned to thank him; he began to say something, but it was too late. A fist swung like a lump hammer out of the darkness and drove into his jaw. His head rang; in the same second he heard the snap of a molar and tasted blood in his mouth; stars burst inside his skull.

# 13

At first, Newton thought he must be lying in the road. He stared up into the morning mist. Concerned voices carried on a conversation over his head; faces peered down at him, but he couldn't tell who was speaking. Why didn't they help him up? Then he realized the air was warm against his face. Time must have passed; if it wasn't for the mist he would be staring up into sunshine. He was shocked that hours could have gone by while he had lain there, although right now he couldn't quite remember what had happened. He just knew that the last time he had had his eyes open it was night.

The sensation was not unpleasant, lying here in the mist. Inside his head, Newton smiled to himself. He could just stay here. Why not? The sound of the voices was comforting; it was strange that they were close and yet he couldn't make out what they were saying. Why was that? The question wheeled round in his head. He wanted to speak, to ask how he came to be here, to know why no one had helped him up, to find out how long he had lain like this. But the effort of thinking of the words and then making them in his mouth was too much. He had no strength, not even the energy to ask.

'Inspector?'

Newton recognized a voice. Inspector. Someone was speaking to him. He had the strange sensation that he had forgotten who he was; the voice made him remember. He just couldn't see who was speaking, the mist was too thick.

'Inspector?'

The same voice. He wished he could place it; whoever it was knew him.

Newton tried to lever himself up on his elbow. It was ridiculous to just lie here. He'd ask one of them to help him up. As soon as he moved, a great stone rolled inside his head; blinding pain exploded as if a sledgehammer caught him on the back of the skull. He lay back. The voices above him were saying something.

'Inspector?'

Abigail's face leaned down through the mist. She was smiling at him. It was such a relief that she was here, so good to see her smile. He wanted her to help him up. Why was she letting him lie here?

Then he remembered. That was it. He had to tell her something, something urgent, something he had been meaning to tell her for a long time. He would tell her now. In his head he searched for whatever it was but couldn't find it. What was it that was so important? For the life of him, he couldn't say.

'Can you hear me?'

Abigail's voice made him feel calm; it reassured him like a familiar tune which he had not heard for a long time. But why was she asking such an odd question? Of course he could hear her. She was telling him to lie still, not to move; he had hit his head when he fell. He heard her words but they did not quite make sense, almost as if she was talking about somebody else, not him. Newton nodded. The stone rolled inside his head again.

He had to lie still. He had no choice. He had to close his eyes. The sound of the voices retreated into the mist. For a second, Newton believed he was on a boat which had slipped its mooring and was gently carried out on the tide; the voices drifted away. As sleep over-took him, he could hear Abigail; it warmed his heart to know she was there.

★ ★ ★

Newton woke abruptly. The room was full of sunlight. Outside the window were daytime sounds: the rumble of cartwheels and the clatter of horses' hoofs on cobbles, voices, laughter, the screech of gulls.

The room was not familiar to him. The ceiling was low and the casement gave a view of the blue sky. Gradually, he took stock of his surroundings. He was in bed, wearing a nightshirt. His suit had been neatly arranged on a hanger which hung from the picture rail on the opposite wall. Beside him on a table stood a glass of milk and a plate containing a hunk of bread and a piece of yellow cheese. The sight of the cheese reminded him he was starving; it seemed like he hadn't eaten for days. Despite the banging in his head, he levered himself up. Eating with a raging pain in one side of his jaw, the salty cheese was the most mouth-watering thing he had ever tasted, rich and sharp. The crust of the bread cracked between his fingers; the crumb was soft and sweet.

The bedroom door opened cautiously.

'You gave us a scare, sir.'

Culley pulled a chair up beside the bed.

'My orders are to see you lie still.'

He passed Newton the glass of milk and watched him sip it.

'Where am I?'

'Don't you know?' Culley laughed. 'Upstairs at the Newfoundland.'

226

Newton lay back while Culley outlined what had happened.

'Constable Lamb found you in a lane leading out to the skern, picked you up and carried you back here across his shoulders. Someone gave you a right one. You fell back and cracked your head. Miss March says she'll be surprised if you remember anything about it. Tell you one thing though, whoever it was took your gun.'

Newton groaned. A picture formed in his head, men with a lantern kneeling in the road.

'There were two of them.'

Culley was leaning over him as if he had to strain to catch what Newton was saying.

'Where's Abigail?' Newton said.

'Miss March will be right along,' Culley announced. 'She and Mrs Hookway are making broth.'

Newton lay back. Jigsaw pieces were in his head but he couldn't make a picture.

'Your watch was still in your pocket.' Culley tried to cheer him up.

'The letter,' Newton said. 'That's why I went out there.'

'You mean this?'

Culley produced a sheet of paper from his pocket. Dry now, the writing had washed away; the ink had separated into a rainbow of blue and pink.

'It was in your pocket, but you'd been lying in a ditch. You were soaked through.'

A piece of jigsaw clicked into place.

'Norman.' Newton struggled to remember what the note had said. 'Someone was warning us off.'

'You're supposed to be resting.' Culley looked grave. 'I'm under strict instructions.'

'Has he turned up?'

'Rest,' Culley said. 'Close your eyes for a while. Miss March will be bringing you up some broth.'

Newton sank back into his pillow. The day was bright outside the window; knots in the glass drew curls in the sky. He could smell food being prepared downstairs; hunger gnawed at him. The jigsaw pieces moved around inside his head. Sometimes he recognized part of a picture, at other times nothing made sense.

Culley crossed the room, held the sheet of paper flat against the window and peered at it.

'Boy?' Culley said. 'Could that be one of the words?'

Newton didn't know. How could he remember?

'Not to worry,' Culley went on brightly. 'There's a train in the morning, provided you're back on your feet.'

The jigsaw pieces scattered again. Culley took a chair from the bedside, parked it by the window, rested his feet on the sill and settled down to stare out at the quay. Whenever Newton tried to say anything, he shushed him. Miss March insisted he rest, he said; he wasn't supposed to be talking at all.

Newton gave up. He stared at the back of Culley's head and struggled to remember what the letter had said. The smell of food from downstairs slipped through the cracks in the floorboards and under the door. The voices of men below him in the parlour bar rose and fell like waves. The pain in Newton's head settled to a dull ache. He gingerly explored the side of his swollen face with the tips of his fingers and felt round the inside of his mouth with his tongue. He could feel the sharp edge of a broken tooth; he could taste blood. Outside the window, the stabbing cries of the gulls reminded him of something; there was no point in asking Culley.

When Abigail pushed open the door, the first thing Newton said was, 'What happened in Exeter?'

Abigail beamed at him and held the door for Lizzie Hookway, who carried in a tray of steaming broth and a mound of fresh bread.

'Exactly what the doctor ordered,' she said brightly.

The two women plumped his pillows while Culley sat him up. Lizzie Hookway settled the tray containing chicken broth and hunks of bread on his knees and as Newton took his first few mouthfuls, she saw to the fire. Abigail came and sat beside him and laughed good-naturedly as he struggled with the spoon; one side of his mouth wouldn't work. Culley stood by the window.

When Newton had cleaned the plate and Lizzie Hookway taken the tray, he turned to Abigail. Her smile disappeared. Her skin seemed to lose its colour; the bones in her face were sharp.

'We were too late. The storm brought a tree down across the line. We had to put up in Crediton overnight.'

Abigail hesitated while she brushed away tears. She looked towards the window; outside, the gulls wheeled. Newton had never seen her lose her composure like this. She steadied herself on the edge of her chair and turned towards him.

'Edward took his own life in his cell that first evening.' Her voice fell to a whisper. She stared down at her lap; her fingers plucked at the material of her skirt.

'He had no one to speak for him. He must have been overtaken by despair.' She found a handkerchief and brushed the tears from her eyes. 'I called on the prosecuting counsel in his chambers. He talked about justice; he said there was a confession.' She turned and stared at Newton. 'He had to sort through his papers before he remembered Edward's name.'

The ache in Newton's head threatened to split his skull in two; he pulled himself upright. Abigail stared out at the gulls again.

'I have searched for Norman,' she said. 'The station, the quay, I've been to his house. No one has seen him since the day before yesterday. Westcott said he sent him on an errand and hasn't seen him since. He says he left with you . . . '

'Two days?' Newton grabbed the sheets in his fists. 'How long have I been like this?'

'It's Saturday, sir,' Culley said. 'Friday came and went. It seemed a shame to wake you.'

'A good long sleep,' Abigail said. 'You needed it. Another day or two in bed and you'll be as right as rain. You'll have a few bruises and you may need to visit a dentist but — '

'This is ridiculous. Leave the room, if you please. I wish to get dressed.' Newton threw back the blankets. The ball rolled inside his skull. 'And you,' he snapped at Culley. 'What are you doing here? Have the weapons been found?'

'Sir Lawrence's orders are that we leave on the next train,' Culley protested.

'To hell with Sir Lawrence,' Newton's voice tore at his throat. 'And his damn orders.'

Everything was back in focus; Newton swung his legs over the side of the bed. The sudden movement made the ache inside his skull burst into flames. He remembered the letter which told him not to look for Norman; he remembered two men struggling to mend a broken wheel.

'Are the rifles found?' Newton was insistent.

'I went out to the skern with the constables and watched the boats sail on the tide.' Culley tried to explain. 'None of them doubled back. None of them made for any of the bays. We would have seen.'

'They knew you were there. They decided to leave the guns where they are.' Newton's temper boiled. He ignored the pain in his skull and rounded on Abigail. 'Miss March, will you leave the room so I may put on my trousers?'

'You have had a blow to the head,' Abigail insisted. 'You should rest while your strength returns.'

'Miss March.' Newton's voice was steel.

Abigail got to her feet.

'Hand me my trousers now.' Newton glared at Culley. 'The rifles have not been moved by sea; they have not been moved by the railway;

a cart bearing their weight would not get ten yards down these lanes before getting stuck in the mud. They are still here.'

'We should first be concerned about Norman.' Abigail's hand was on the door handle. 'I have to inform him.'

'We shall find him. We shall find the rifles,' Newton said. 'We shall not rest until we do.'

As Culley unhooked the suit from the picture rail, Abigail slipped out of the room.

'How did Lamb find me?' Newton's mind raced. He ignored the concussion pains in the back of his head. 'I must have been a mile outside town.'

'He says you called him,' Culley said. 'He followed you.'

Newton remembered the light from a night-watch lantern as he stepped out into the street.

'That was Lamb?' Newton said.

Something was wrong. Something was staring him in the face.

'Did he assault me?'

Culley didn't understand.

'He followed you. He came upon you lying in a ditch by the side of the lane. He picked you up and carried you back here, hammered on the door until the barman let him in.'

'Did he identify the men?'

Culley looked blank.

'I surprised two men in the lane. Their cart lost a wheel.'

'He made no mention of anyone,' Culley said. 'Maybe they had gone.'

'One of them must have hit me,' Newton said.

'Would you recognize them again?' Culley said.

'It was pitch dark; the lantern gave little light.'

Newton made his way over to the washstand and poured water from a china jug into the bowl. It felt odd to be on his feet again; the floor lurched as if it was the deck of a boat. The soap stung his eyes; he could barely touch the side of his face without wincing.

'Have you been out to the farm again?'

'I persuaded Molland to let me search the house and the barns.' Culley sighed. 'I rode out to where the *Brianna* was blown ashore. I walked the fields where he keeps his sheep; I looked for disturbed earth, any signs that anything had been buried.'

Newton nodded.

'Molland still maintains he lit the barrels, Gypsies overturned them and caused the wreck.'

'There are no Gypsies,' Newton said. 'Rawle says Molland complains about everything.'

'I went over the place. Constable Lamb was with me.'

'Lamb?'

'He knows it well. His father worked out there until there was a falling-out. Molland was not pleased to see him. He would have thrown him off the land if I had not insisted.'

'We have to find the boy,' Newton said. 'The constables won't spend their time looking for him. Miss March will not wish to leave unless she sees him.'

'Sir.' Culley looked pained. 'Sir Lawrence insists we return to London by the next train. He says I am to see to it. It is not our job to look for a runaway orphan.'

'Sir Lawrence may have changed his mind,' Newton snapped. 'We have not yet carried out our duty.'

Newton gently soaped his swollen face in front of the mirror. Discoloured flesh too sensitive to touch bulged on one side of his jaw. One eye was bloodshot and his jaw clicked. Even when he kept his tongue well away from the broken molar, he still tasted blood. On the back of his head, he discovered an egg-shaped swelling beneath matted hair. It felt as if someone was holding a hot iron an inch away from his skull; the sensation of burning threatened to blossom into pain. When he pulled on his jacket with the Webley gone from his pocket, it felt too light.

At the foot of the stairs, Abigail ambushed him.

'You should not be out of bed, Inspector.' She looked him straight in the eye. 'You have suffered a concussion. If I were a male doctor and ordered you to stay in bed, you would do so.'

'I can assure you, I would not.' Newton's mouth twisted in an attempt at good humour. 'But I am grateful for your concern.'

Abigail did not smile. She noticed the way Newton kept hold of the newel post and how white his face was around the swelling.

Newton beckoned her towards the table in the window. Culley joined them.

'Where is Constable Lamb now?' Newton said.

'Walking his beat in the town,' Culley said. 'Where else would he be?'

'Do you trust him?' Newton kept his voice low.

'Why shouldn't I?' Culley looked puzzled.

'He's always there.' Abigail was one step ahead. 'He found Catalin on the boat; he arrested poor Edward; he found you in the lane.'

'I was out on the cliffs with him all night.' Culley appealed to Newton. 'He showed me everything, back lanes, short cuts across the fields. When he was a boy, his father worked the lime kiln out at the Molland farm.'

Outside, the quay was almost empty. A few pedestrians sauntered past, making the most of the end of a bright afternoon. At the head of one of the slipways, a carriage waited for fares, the driver slumped half-asleep in his seat. The tide was out. Gulls pecked for lugworms; their spotless white and grey feathers shone against the brown skin of river mud and the blackened columns of the bridge. Nests of flotsam rested between the arches; bleached sticks, tangled seaweed, old planks torn from wrecked hulls all awaited the next tide.

'Tell me about this Irish boat,' Newton said. 'The one that carried the guns.'

'What can I tell you?' Culley glanced at Abigail.

'I am not moving from the inspector's side,' Abigail said flatly. 'He is my patient.'

'Tell me why it sailed from a village on Sir Lawrence's estate,' Newton said.

'How can I answer that?' Culley laughed. 'There are boats in every town along that coast. The men there have fished since the beginning of time.'

'The boat came from Sir Lawrence's estate; you were appointed to come down here by Sir Lawrence over the heads of Scotland

Yard.' Abigail spoke quietly as if she were ticking things off on a list. 'You're suggesting this is a coincidence, Sergeant?'

'I explained all this to the inspector.' Culley looked away; if Newton had not been there, he would have refused to answer. 'My family have lived on his estate for generations. He helped us. He helped me. What are you insinuating?' Culley dug his heels in the floor and shoved his chair back. 'We should be back in London, that's all I know, not wasting time doing the work of the local constables.'

'Quite a coincidence,' Newton said. 'You have to admit that.'

'Yes, it is a coincidence.' Culley leaned forward as if he was just about to jump up from his seat. 'What do you want me to say?'

'The missing boy,' Newton said. 'During your night on the cliff tops, did Constable Lamb mention him?'

'I pressed him,' Culley said. 'Of course I did. Did he know anywhere the boy might have gone? Did he know of any relatives? Did he have any friends?'

'And?'

'And the answer was he lived with his brother and if it wasn't for the stationmaster needing someone to run errands, both of them would be in the workhouse.' Culley folded his arms in front of him. 'And all the better for it, if you ask me; the one would still be alive and the other wouldn't be missing.'

'Back home, we send orphan children to work on farms,' Abigail said fiercely. 'The families treat them as one of their own; the boys help the farmer, girls help with the indoor work. We do not lock them away in workhouses. It is a scheme advocated by the new government of which my father is a member.'

Newton was suddenly aware that their voices had attracted the attention of the drinkers at the bar.

'I want you to call in at the police station.' Newton turned to Culley. 'Tell Constable Lamb to find me. Then proceed to the railway station to see if Westcott has heard from Norman.'

Culley was about to protest and then thought better of it. He smiled briefly at Abigail and stood up.

'I should like some fresh air.' Newton levered himself to his feet. Now his mind was focused, the pain in his head subsided to a dull ache. 'A walk across the bridge would do me good.'

'Inspector, I really think . . . ' Abigail began.

Once outside, they could see the colour of the river mud deepen as the afternoon light paled; shadows gathered in the narrow streets, filled the drangways and collected beneath the arches of the bridge. Warmth slipped out of the air. Sensing a turn in the tide, the gulls took off from the flats in the centre of the river, wheeled over the town and headed down the sweep of the estuary where the first fishing boats would appear.

'I visited the vicarage,' Abigail said. 'The girl is recovering well. All she needs is good food and rest. Poor Mrs Dauncy is doing her best, but she has a propensity for feeling put upon. I am afraid she will lose patience and turf her out at any time.'

'Were you able to speak to the girl?'

'Oh yes,' Abigail said playfully. 'And she to me. The problem was that neither one of us was able to understand the other.'

As Newton laughed his jaw clicked and needled him with pain.

'That's better, Inspector.' Abigail smiled at him. 'Laughter helps keep your spirits up and that enables you to overcome your difficulties. I tried the same thing with Mrs Dauncy, but with less success.'

They walked on a few yards in silence. They were close enough to hear shouts of the men from the boatyard. Caulkers worked their way round the hull of the vessel in dry dock; smoke from a wood fire columned upwards and the air smelled of tar.

'Perhaps Norman could be taken on at one of the yards,' Newton said. 'He is an intelligent boy. There must be someone who could find a trade for him.'

'I didn't realize you had a concern for his welfare.' Abigail looked at him.

'Running errands for Westcott is all that stands between him and the Board of Guardians.' Newton shrugged. 'If the Reverend Dauncy had his way he would be in the workhouse now.'

Newton stared out over the river. The tide had turned; incoming rivulets twisted like liquid rope between the mud-flats, spilling over the existing channels and gouging new ones where there were none before.

'Norman is fond of you,' Newton said.

'Poor Norman,' Abigail said modestly. 'He is fond of anyone who spares him a kind word.'

'You have a way with him,' Newton insisted. 'I noticed it.'

They reached the end of the bridge and turned back. Colour had drained from the western sky and the light faded over the town; already, there were lamps alight in some of the windows along the quay. As the door to the Newfoundland opened and shut, lamplight the colour of beeswax shone on the cobbles.

'Miss March,' Newton said suddenly. 'I

have something to say to you.'

Something in the urgency of his voice made Abigail draw in a sharp breath as though she had touched her fingers on a stove. She said nothing and allowed him to take his time. This should have made it easier for him; instead, Newton felt the muscles tighten across his shoulders. His mouth dried.

'The first morning we were here, while you were recovering at the Newfoundland Inn . . .'

Why was this so hard? He considered himself an honest man and all he wished was to be honest; he wanted to be frank with Abigail so that there were no secrets between them. He had been brought up to be a gentleman and had been taught that this meant doing what was right. Now he found that good manners meant keeping secrets and formality disguised the facts. Nothing had prepared him for this: to speak to someone as an equal and to tell the truth.

'A child was abandoned in my hotel room.' He blurted out the words, barely in control of what he was saying. 'An infant, a foundling. I was angry; I took it as a slur on my character. I was offended because I believed people would suspect I had fathered the child and that my reputation would be compromised. I lacked all sympathy. I told the manager I wanted nothing to do with it.'

'Inspector.' Abigail lightly rested her hand on his arm.

'I was embarrassed; I was not frank with you, Miss March.'

Newton searched her face to see how his words affected her.

'What should I fear from a defenceless child?' He smiled bitterly. 'Dauncy has arranged for it to be sent to the workhouse; there is a nursing mother who can look after it.'

He paused, expecting her to reply. When she was silent, more of the story spilled out of him; he wanted to tell her everything.

'Culley says the mother came forward when she heard the child was to be sent to the workhouse. She is the sister of Constable Lamb; it seems he put her up to this. She has pleaded with Dauncy to get the child released from the workhouse back into her care.'

Although there was still light in the sky, shadows collected in the streets and doorways across the town. Voices carried; shouts and laughter echoed from the doorway of the Newfoundland Inn. Water flowed over the mudbanks in the centre of the river; the screech of gulls announced the turn of the tide.

'I did not feel I could tell you,' Newton said. 'I should have taken pity on the child.'

'You could have told me.' Abigail smiled at

him and turned to walk back across the bridge. Newton kept pace alongside her. 'What difference would it have made? The infant was abandoned. Ordering the hotel manager to find a home for it was all you could do. Poor Charlotte had not announced herself then.'

'Charlotte?' Newton said. 'You know the girl's name.'

'It has been the main topic of conversation in the parlour bar for the past two nights,' Abigail said.

'Then you knew.' Newton felt ridiculous.

'I am honoured that you think enough of me to tell me the tale yourself, Inspector,' Abigail said. 'Full of physical strength and bravery they may be, but many men are strangers to moral courage.'

Abigail turned to him.

'I see that you are not.'

The compliment brought colour to Newton's face. The sense of relief he felt at having told her was dizzying.

'You will be pleased to know that Dauncy has requested the Board of Guardians to return the child to Charlotte. There was disagreement as some members considered Charlotte's father might be a danger to the child so they deferred a decision. But dear Lizzie has offered to take Charlotte on as a servant girl. She has undertaken to provide bed and board and a small wage with one day off a month after a trial period.' Abigail smiled warmly. 'Mother and child will be able to live at the Newfoundland Inn if the Board agrees.'

'I understand Constable Lamb put her up to it,' Newton said.

'The poor girl was desperate; she is not to be blamed. Her father was on the point of throwing her out; she had to find a home for the child or give herself up to the workhouse.'

While Newton shared Abigail's sympathy for the girl, he knew that every time Lamb's name came up something was wrong. Abigail herself had pointed this out. Of all the men in Bideford, why had Lamb encouraged his sister to leave the infant in his room? He knew what Rawle's reaction would be when word reached him.

'There he is now,' Abigail said suddenly; she pointed towards the inn door. 'I'll wager he's looking for you.'

Constable Lamb stepped out of the New-foundland Inn doorway, squared his shoulders, clasped his hands behind him and began to pace with the slow, self-conscious strides of the Watch. Anyone in his path moved out of the way.

'He knows every one of these people and they all know him, yet he greets no one and no one speaks to him,' Newton said.

Lamb stopped suddenly. Something caught his attention in an alley between the buildings. The shrill blast of his whistle cut the evening air. Passers-by stopped and stared. Then someone dashed out of the alley, kept his head low and threaded through the crowd like a shadow. He was fast. A few people made attempts to grab him, but he jinxed left and right out of reach. There were shouts. People pointed. Yards behind, Lamb gave chase. He gave a second blast on his whistle; he was already losing ground.

The runaway cut the corner and launched himself on to the bridge, leaving Lamb pounding along the quay. Newton and Abigail stood directly in his path. As he closed pell-mell on them, they saw who it was. No cap, hair wild, face and clothes black as a sweep's boy, he tore down the centre of the bridge as if dogs were at his heels.

'Norman,' Abigail called; she stretched her arms wide.

Norman skidded to a halt in front of her. He glanced over his shoulder. Lamb was on the bridge. There was a third shrill stab from his whistle; somewhere, another constable answered. The boy's eyes were wild; tears cut tracks in the dirt on his face; his hands were balled into fists. He stared up at Abigail.

'Did they hang him, miss?'

# 14

Abigail clasped the boy round his shoulders and drew him to her; she held him tight for a second before he pushed her away. Black dirt from his clothes rubbed off on her jacket and skirt.

'Did they, miss?' He appealed to her.

'Norman . . . ' Abigail began.

He glanced back over his shoulder. Lamb was halfway across the bridge, running hard; he pointed at them and shouted. People turned to look.

'We should go somewhere and talk.'

Abigail tried to keep her composure. Silent tears broke in Norman's eyes and flooded his dirty cheeks; he stared up at her.

Then Lamb was there, face burning, furious, out of breath. He clutched his side with one hand and made a grab for Norman with the other. The boy twisted out of reach, ducked round behind Abigail and clung to her skirt. Newton blocked Lamb's way.

'This young whippersnapper.' Lamb struggled to catch his breath. 'I'm taking him with me.'

'I need to speak to him, Constable,' Abigail announced. 'I am keeping him with me.'

'Madam, I'm taking him to the station. He's been giving us the runaround. The superintendent wants to see him and give him a dressing-down.'

'You expect me to stand by while you lock a child in a police cell?' Abigail was incensed.

Lamb made another grab; Norman ducked away.

'Enough, Constable,' Newton thundered. 'You heard what Miss March said. The boy is in our safe keeping.'

'He's a little rogue,' Lamb sneered. 'He's pulling the wool over your eyes, the pair of you,' Lamb said. 'You don't want to believe anything he tells you. He's a liar and a thief.'

'I ain't.' Norman peered round from behind Abigail. His eyes were wet with tears. 'You're the liar. You arrested Edward when it wasn't even him that did it. You knew that.'

Lamb made another grab.

'Constable.' Newton blocked his way.

'Out of my way, if you please, sir.' Lamb stood upright; he had recovered his breath. 'I must take this boy with me.'

Norman ducked behind Abigail again, but Lamb was too quick this time. When he appeared round the other side of her, Lamb was ready. He clamped his huge hand round Norman's skinny arm and dragged him out.

Norman flailed his other arm, launched

kicks at Lamb's shins, twisted and pulled, but Lamb held him as if he was manacled.

'See how he protests,' Lamb jeered. 'Sign of a guilty conscience. See how there is no chance of him coming quietly.' He shook Norman violently. 'Have to drag you to the station, won't I?'

'Exactly what do you want him for, Constable?' Abigail tried to pour oil on the situation.

Lamb seized Norman with his other hand and held him at arm's length to avoid the furious kicks the boy was aiming at him.

'See what I've got to deal with?' Lamb was triumphant.

Spectators gathered; men and women pushed forward to see what was going on. At first, the spectacle of a town constable seizing a ne'er-do-well, who was clearly guilty to judge by the struggle he was putting up, was irresistible.

'You all know this urchin,' Lamb announced. 'You know how he steals coal from the station-master and goes begging on the quay. He deserves to be taught a lesson.' Lamb caught the eye of people he knew in the crowd. 'These good folks from London have been taken in. They believe he's an innocent.'

As soon as people recognized Abigail, the crowd quietened; a whisper went round that it was the woman from the river. They stood back from her respectfully. They saw that she was not in the least concerned by the dirt Norman had left on her expensive jacket; they saw the sympathy in her eyes as she looked at the boy struggling to get free from the constable. This was not the reaction Lamb expected; he looked confused. A glazed smile sloped across his face like an angler showing off his catch.

'Miss, miss.' Norman appealed to Abigail. 'You ain't told me.'

Lamb started to drag Norman back down the bridge. As Lamb pushed his way through, the crowd was uneasy. There were catcalls, shouts of 'Let him go' and 'What's he done to you?'. They all knew Constable Lamb and what he was capable of.

'Did they hang him, miss?' Norman tried to wriggle free.

'Shut up, you.' Lamb let go with one of his meaty hands and cuffed the boy across the cheek. Aware that he was still the focus of attention, the grin sat on his mouth. The sound of the slap cracked like a whip.

'Did they, miss?' Norman ignored the pain. 'Tell me, miss.' He kept his eyes on Abigail.

'He is dead, Norman.' Her words fell like stones.

It took a second for the crowd to realize

what Abigail was telling him, a split second for Lamb to realize. Then Lamb laughed. His fist tightened on Norman's shoulder; he swung his hand back for a second clout.

'See what I'm dealing with?' he scoffed. 'His brother's hung for a murder.'

'It ain't true,' Norman screamed. 'It ain't true. Tell 'em, miss.'

'I said shut up, didn't I?' Lamb's second swipe caught Norman across the side of the head.

'Constable.' Newton pushed the onlookers aside. 'I will take the boy. He will be under my charge.'

'Can't expect me to release him, sir.' Lamb looked for support at the crowd. 'I've only just caught the wretch.'

Norman swung a wild kick at his shin, but couldn't reach.

'He'll cool his heels for a few hours and when he's calmed down I'll wheel him in front of the superintendent.'

'It's him,' Norman said suddenly. 'He was the man on the quay you asked me about.'

'The night the girl was killed?' Newton said. 'You're saying Constable Lamb was there?'

'He never done it,' Norman cried, 'but he was there, stood on the quay watching.'

'What's this?' Lamb brayed. 'Are you

making up accusations now?'

The crowd shrank back. Through the dirt, a red welt appeared on the side of Norman's face.

'Release him, Constable. That is an order.'

Lamb's grin crumpled round his mouth.

'I take my orders from Superintendent Rawle, sir.' He squared his shoulders and glared at Newton. 'He ordered me to find this young ruffian and apprehend him.'

Norman threw himself on the ground, forcing Lamb to bend double to hang on to him; then he squirmed between Lamb's legs. Lamb had to let go. Before he could turn and make another grab, Norman scrambled to his feet and cannoned headlong into whoever stood in his way.

Desperate to get away, hardly knowing in which direction he was headed, Norman butted through a row of onlookers and then shouldered past a woman who blocked his path. She screamed as he knocked her off her feet. It was Abigail.

'Miss, miss.' Realizing what he had done, Norman stopped and pulled her up. 'Sorry, miss.'

With an almighty yell, Lamb fell on him. Newton stood in the way. The crowd closed on Lamb like a wall and blocked his path. In the time it took for him to barge through,

Norman was away like a minnow through weeds.

Lamb pulled his whistle out of his pocket and blew two long screeching blasts.

'Does that little guttersnipe think he can get away from me?' Lamb roared. 'He's gone for refuge at the station. Does he think that dawcock stationmaster can save him? I shall have him as soon as another constable arrives. He'll be black and blue before I've finished with him.'

The crowd stared coldly at him. Lamb's anger was ugly. He concentrated on brushing down his uniform and avoided catching anyone's eye. He knew where Norman was headed and, when a second constable arrived, knew he was sure to catch him. He saved face by declaring loudly that there was nothing more to see, turned towards the onlookers and spread his arms wide to marshal them out of the way of a carriage which wound down the hill from the station. The crowd pressed themselves against the bridge parapet and stared out at the rising tide. The reflection of the lights along the quay danced on the water. The first of the boats would soon be in.

As the carriage passed, Abigail caught Newton's arm. Culley peered at them out of the window; in the seat beside him, back amongst the shadows was Norman's dirty face.

⋆ ⋆ ⋆

'Where?'

Ten minutes later, Newton leaned across the table in the Newfoundland Inn. Norman clutched a cold mutton chop in one hand and a crust of bread in the other. Abigail sat beside him while Culley kept watch at the window.

'Dunno the name of it.' Norman demolished the meat first. 'I could take you there. They shut me in a lime kiln. I had to escape through the chimney.'

'You say it was near the sea and there was another building there, a storehouse of some kind?'

'The kiln ain't used.' Norman sucked the mutton bone. 'They keep boxes in it now.'

'Boxes?' Newton said.

'Crates,' Norman said. 'Full of guns.'

Newton, Culley and Abigail all stared at him.

'What?' Norman dropped his bone on the plate. 'They ain't no good. They're all dirty and rusted up.'

'Rifles?' Newton had to be sure. 'You saw them?'

'I only had a look.' Norman waited for

them to accuse him of something. 'I didn't steal them or nothing.'

'That's all right,' Abigail reassured him. 'You've done well.'

She prodded Newton under the table with the toe of her boot.

'Yes, you have,' Newton said quickly. 'And you said there's another building there, a storehouse of some kind?'

'That's a madhouse,' Norman announced grandly. 'There are mad people in it. I spied on 'em through a crack in the door.'

'What kind of mad people?' Abigail said cautiously.

'Women.' Norman stuffed the last of the crust into his mouth.

'And how do you know they are mad?'

'Obvious.' Revived by the food, Norman was full of confidence. 'They were babbling on to each other; none of it made any sense.'

'And they were locked in?' Newton said. 'You're sure?'

'Padlock on the door,' Norman said. 'I saw it.'

'And two men took you there?' Newton carried on. 'What were they like?'

'One was young and one was old. I've seen 'em before, but I don't know their names.' He stared down at his empty plate.

'Sir.' Culley marched across from the

window. 'Two constables on the bridge.'

'You must take us there now.' Newton pushed his chair back and stood up.

'It is almost dark.' Abigail rested her hand lightly on Norman's shoulder. 'Will you be able to find your way?'

Newton shepherded Norman outside to where the line of carriages waited for fares. Culley spoke to one of the drivers, hoisted Norman up to sit beside him and climbed up himself.

'Miss March.' Newton held the carriage door closed. 'I must ask you to wait here.'

'What?' The smile fell from Abigail's face.

'I insist.' Newton looked grave. 'There may be danger. Culley and I must see to it.'

'Danger?' Abigail sounded as though she hadn't quite heard him. 'You are taking the boy.'

'He will wait in the carriage once we have found the place.'

'He says there are women there.'

'Miss March, I am charged with your safety. I cannot knowingly . . . '

'Sir.' Culley leaned down from beside the driver. 'The constables.'

'Very well, Inspector.' Abigail smiled politely. 'You must do as you see fit.'

Newton was surprised at how suddenly she gave in. He nodded briefly and climbed inside. As the coachman clicked his tongue and the carriage lurched forward, Abigail had already turned away.

They turned up the High Street and immediately slowed at the steepness of the hill. The shops were locked and dark, but there was yellow lamplight in the windows of the upper floors where the shopkeepers had their lodgings. The street was almost deserted; what few pedestrians there were stopped to stare at Norman and Culley perched up on top of the coach.

For an hour, the route wound along narrow lanes bordered by high hedges. Eventually, the carriage drew up in a yard surrounded by trees. There was a bite in the air; from close by came the unending rumble of the sea. The moon cast a silver light over a lime kiln and a low stone building roofed in slate. From the far end of the yard, a steep track led down the combe to a jetty where breakers reared and dashed themselves on the rocks. Offshore, moonlight caught the white caps of the waves as they fractured under the swell.

'Don't know what brings you out here.' The driver leaned down to Newton. 'This place ain't never been used proper. A few years ago the farmer took it into his head to make his own lime. Didn't reckon on how difficult it would be hauling the stone up from the jetty.'

'Is this all there is?' Newton said.

'There's a cottage where the burners used to live half a mile across the fields; it's deserted now.'

Newton borrowed one of the carriage lanterns and followed Culley over to the kiln. The fat funnel was stone built; moss and weeds grew where the mortar should have been. The draw hole at the base was blocked and wedged tightly.

'See what they did?' Norman inched the smaller stones out of the draw hole and flung them across the yard. 'They were going to leave me in here.'

'You said you'd seen them before.'

Newton's arms burned as he helped Culley lever out a block of limestone.

'On the boat,' Norman said. 'The two of them. That constable was on the quay.'

He kicked at the stone in the draw hole.

'You won't let them take me, will you?' Another note sounded in his voice. 'I've helped you, ain't I? I've shown you where this place is?'

'We won't let them take you,' Newton reassured him. 'What do you mean on the boat?'

'That night,' Norman said. 'I told you. They cut that girl's throat. The constable was on the quay.'

In the flickering lantern light, Newton saw

how thin and small Norman was; his face and clothes were filthy; he looked exhausted. He twisted the edge of his jacket in his fingers. By showing them this place, he had played all his cards. For a moment, Newton thought he might turn and run.

'I've told you everything now.' Norman looked up at him.

'I'm grateful for it,' Newton said.

'The guns are in there.' Norman pointed to the draw hole. His voice shook. 'I ain't going in again. You'll have to fetch 'em out if you want 'em.'

Between them, Culley and Newton heaved a block of stone away and cleared a hole big enough to crawl through. Culley took the lantern and went first.

Inside, the walls were soot black and so thick they deadened all sound; for the first time since they'd got to the area, the sea became inaudible. Over their heads was a circle of the night sky; beneath their feet, the dirt floor was strewn with wood ash and lumps of limestone. Right in front of them were the five long crates Newton had seen in the police cell; they were untidily stacked, obviously having been dumped in a hurry. The lid on the top one was loose. When Culley lifted it and held up the lantern, they saw a row of Enfields. They were dirty; mud clung to the barrels.

'Buried and dug up,' Culley said. 'What did I tell you?'

'Why did no one clean them?' Newton said. 'They're useless like this.'

'Sometimes they stay buried for years. Someone cleans them when they need to use them.'

'We'll need help moving them,' Newton said.

Culley handed him the lantern and started to crawl back through the draw hole. When he got to the other side, Newton expected him to reach back in for the light, but he didn't. As Newton inched forward on his hands and knees, he felt the cold night air on his face and heard the sound of the sea again. He called out to Culley to take the lantern, but there was no answer. As he pushed forward, the candle guttered.

Newton crawled through the final part of the opening on his elbows, levered himself to his feet and came face to face with two men. Culley lay on the ground a few feet away; his eyes were closed.

'You again?'

There were two of them, an older man, grey-haired with a split in the shoulder seam of his coat; a dark-haired younger man. In the second he saw the old man swing his club,

Newton crooked his arm across his face and launched himself forward. The club sang past his ear and cracked down on his shoulder. The pain gouged the breath out of him. As he fell on his face, they grabbed him.

'It's that London policeman,' one of them shouted.

The men wrenched Newton's arms up behind his back, almost dislocating them from their sockets.

'Tie him up.'

One of them knelt on his back while the other trussed his arms and tied his ankles tightly.

'What are we going to do with 'em, Pa?'

'Leave 'em. By the time somebody finds 'em, we'll be miles away.'

Newton lifted his face out of the cold mud; he heard Culley groan. The carriage which brought them had disappeared. Newton's brain somersaulted. Had they just packed the driver off back to town? What about Norman? Newton had a vision of him slipping as quick as a fish through the crowds on the bridge; dodging these two oafs would be no problem.

Newton lay still. He watched the men check the knots which held Culley, turn away and trudge across the yard. One of them slipped behind the stone building. A minute later he appeared again, leading a horse which pulled a high-sided hay cart.

'Just be careful,' the older man snarled. 'Bring 'em out one by one.'

He wrestled with the padlock and when it snapped free, pulled the door open a few feet.

'They ain't gonna run, Pa. We trussed 'em proper.'

'We've already lost one.' The older man held the door ready to slam it shut. 'Thanks to you.'

The young man disappeared into the building. Eventually, he frogmarched a young woman out into the yard and shoved her towards the cart. Clearly terrified, the woman did not protest; her hands were tied. The old man jabbed her with his club. A second woman was brought out. Then a third. They were all barefoot, hands tied; their arms and faces were ingrained with dirt; their dark hair was matted. They looked half-starved. The young man heaved himself up into the back of the cart and forced the women down on to the floor.

Newton shuffled himself nearer Culley and angled himself so he could reach him with the toe of his boot. Culley was swimming in and out of consciousness; in the moonlight, the blood on his face looked black. When Newton nudged him, he didn't respond.

Across the yard, the old man circled the

horse in the direction of the lane. Before setting off, he took a clay pipe from his pocket and turned his back to the wind. The young man settled himself down in the back of the wagon; to a passer-by, the cart would look empty.

'Them's the mad women.'

Newton felt Norman's breath on his ear. He turned to see the boy kneeling over him in the shadows.

'I've got a bit of slate,' Norman whispered.

Newton felt the boy saw at the ropes round his wrist; he heard him catch his breath with the effort of it. When he craned round to look at him, Norman bit his lip with concentration; every now and then he glanced over towards the cart where the old man held his coat up against the wind while he struggled to light his pipe.

'Quietly,' Newton pleaded; Norman's grunts were getting louder.

'I don't care about them,' Norman whispered. 'They'd never catch me.'

Newton strained his wrists against the ropes, but they still held tight.

'Keep still,' Norman insisted.

Across the yard, the old man hauled himself up into the driver's seat, the stub of his clay pipe clenched between his teeth; he dropped his club down beside him. Just as he was ready to shake the reins, he froze. Then he leaned round and hissed something at the man in the back of the cart.

A carriage with its lanterns lit pulled into the yard. The driver called out a whoa and heaved the horses up short.

'You're blocking the road,' the old man snarled. 'Move forward.'

The carriage stayed where it was.

'I said move. What's the matter with you?'

The driver leaned down; somebody was giving him instructions from inside.

For a moment, the old man seemed at a loss. Then he fumbled in the pocket of his coat and produced a short-barrelled pistol, Newton's Webley Bulldog.

'What's going on? Are you deaf, driver?' He waved the gun in the direction of the carriage.

The rope round Newton's wrists suddenly gave. Norman laughed with relief. Trying to make sense of what they heard, the men stopped and stared across at them. Norman started sawing at the rope round Newton's ankles.

'It's that boy.' The young man pointed.

'Move the damn carriage,' the old man roared. 'Us wants to get by.'

Caught between noticing Norman, the carriage and the old man's anger, the younger man hesitated.

'What's the matter with you?' The old man continued to wave the gun. 'Do you want us to shoot you?'

Norman gave a last few violent saws with his slate.

'Put that gun down.' The command was high and sharp.

The young man turned. The old man struggled to cock the pistol; the mechanism was unfamiliar to him. The door to the carriage opened and Abigail stepped down into the yard.

'It's Miss,' Norman whispered excitedly.

'What do you want?' The old man was nonplussed.

'I've come for the women,' Abigail said calmly.

The old man gaped at her. It took him a second to recover himself. He scrambled down from the cart, hurried the few yards across to the carriage and grabbed the bridle of the lead horse.

'I told you to move,' he shouted. 'Get out of my way.'

The young man ran across to help him.

'Stop that,' Abigail shouted.

The young women peered over the tailboard of the cart. With both men hauling on the bridles, the carriage inched forward. The coachman yelled.

Abigail walked calmly towards them. She had on her comfortable brown suit she had worn on the journey down, no hat because it had been lost in the river on that first day and her precious red boots which no longer possessed their store-bought sheen, but still stood up to the mud. In her hand she held her travelling purse. Starting with the old man who stood nearest to her, she stared at each of the men in turn.

'Get out of my way,' the old man growled.

'I shall always be in your way,' Abigail said.

With one hand still clutching the bridle, he swung the Webley so it pointed straight at her; loathing twisted his face. The young man laughed nervously.

'I have warned you,' Abigail said.

'Want a taste of this, do you?' He waved the gun.

From over by the kiln, Newton yelled at her to get out of the way. Distracted for a moment, the men turned. Abigail slipped something out of her purse and held it out; it flashed silver in the moonlight. When the old man faced her again, he may have thought she was offering him money. Still holding the Webley in his outstretched hand, he took a step towards her.

When the shot rang out, the old man stood still and stared in horror at his shoulder. The

Webley slipped from his hand. He looked questioningly at Abigail for a second before his legs gave way under him and he sank to his knees in the mud.

# 15

'Place this man in handcuffs and lock him in the cells.'

Rawle's voice was close to a scream. He was on his feet; anger clawed the blood out of his face. Newton faced him squarely across his desk; the sergeant and Constable Lamb stood on either side of him.

'I tried to stop him coming up here, sir.' The sergeant looked terrified. 'He barged straight past me.'

'I have come to make my report.' Newton glared at Rawle.

'I warned you,' Rawle snapped. 'Now look what has happened.'

'I have come to explain.'

In spite of Newton's efforts to shake himself free, Lamb grabbed his wrist and levered it behind his back while the sergeant snapped the handcuffs shut.

'This is ridiculous.' Inflamed with fury, Newton fought to control himself. 'Let me speak.'

'I know what happened.' Rawle spat out his words. 'Last night, the Canadian shot a local man. If he dies, this will be a murder case.

This woman is under your care. You are responsible.'

'It was self-defence,' Newton snapped. 'The man threatened her with a gun.'

'She shot him,' Rawle roared.

'She transported the man back to the Newfoundland Inn in her own carriage, extracted the bullet herself and sewed up the wound. She made him comfortable and he spent the night in front of the fire. That is hardly the action of someone who intends murder.' Newton struggled to hold on to his temper. 'She is making sure the man is comfortable; she will be along shortly.'

'She will find you in the cells.' Rawle glowered. 'I have telegraphed Scotland Yard. Your career is finished. When this Miss March comes here, I shall decide whether or not she is to be locked up alongside you.'

'Superintendent.' Newton made a massive attempt at reasonableness. 'We have discovered the rifles. We've discovered the foreign women locked in a storehouse and freed them. We have also identified the men responsible.'

'I understand the orphan boy guided you,' Rawle said dismissively.

'The men walled him up in the lime kiln. He escaped through the chimney.'

'These men are Constable Lamb's father and brother,' Rawle said. He caught Lamb's eye. 'What do you have to say about this, Constable?'

'I keep my eye on that boy.' Lamb squared his shoulders. 'He is dishonest on account of having no proper upbringing. As I arrested his brother for murder, I should expect him to be vindictive towards me and my family.'

'Exactly.' Rawle nodded in approval.

'You are saying Norman is making all this up?'

'The word of a 12-year-old orphan is hardly evidence,' Rawle said.

'My sergeant and I can identify the two men.'

Newton took a pace forward closer towards the desk. Lamb and the sergeant grabbed his arms.

'After the *Brianna* was washed ashore, my father and brother found the girls wandering on the skern, babbling in some foreign tongue,' Lamb explained. 'Two of them ran off. They locked the others in the barn for their own safety. They fed them and gave them straw bedding; they gave them what comfort they could.'

Lamb's grip tightened.

'They are poor men; Molland took them on to work at the lime kiln. But he sited it wrong; the land was too steep to haul the stone up from the jetty. All their work building it came to nothing.'

'They tied the girls by the wrists.' Newton was beside himself. 'They held them prisoner.'

'After the wreck, the women were hysterical.' Lamb appealed to Rawle. 'They were incapable of looking after themselves.'

'And what were your father and brother doing out there in the middle of the night?' Newton knew Lamb would have an answer ready. And whatever it was, he knew Rawle would believe him.

'They came to collect the women now they had recovered their strength,' Lamb said. 'They heard that one who ran away from the wreck found her way to the vicarage. They intended to take the others to join her.'

'They knocked the consciousness out of my sergeant,' Newton snapped. 'How do you think I came by these bruises?'

'You appeared from out of the kiln and leapt at them in the dark.' Lamb was the soul of reasonableness. 'They didn't know who you were. They were defending themselves.'

'This is laughable,' Newton protested. 'The men are wreckers. They overturned the farmer's tar barrels in order to lure a boat on to the beach.'

'The *Brianna* lost her mast at sea,' Rawle interrupted. 'The storm washed her on to the skern. Tar barrels have nothing to do with it.'

'When the boat was beached, the crew ran off because their cargo was contraband rifles and these women,' Newton carried on. 'Most likely, they were heading for Liverpool. When they found themselves cast ashore on the Devonshire coast, they took to their heels.' He felt Lamb's grip tighten on his arm. 'Old man Lamb and his son were waiting to help themselves to whatever was in the hold. It is my belief that they were going to sell both the rifles and the women as soon as they could find a buyer.'

'I have heard wild insinuations in my time, Inspector.' Rawle's laugh sounded like a bark. 'These men are lime porters. Do you expect me to believe they are involved in some kind of slave trade?'

'They are wreckers,' Newton insisted. 'Opportunists. As soon as the ship ran aground, whether they lured her or not, they seized the cargo. And that cargo was contraband. It is as plain as day.'

'Take him to the cells,' Rawle snapped. 'Miss March attempted a murder and you as good as put her up to it. The assizes judge will decide what to do with you. As for Miss March, I shall attempt to charge her as well, but as she is the daughter of a guest of a Member of Parliament, I imagine I shall receive orders to let her return to London.'

Lamb and the sergeant attempted to wheel Newton towards the door.

'The boy saw those men kill the girl on the boat.' Newton's words rang like a bell. 'He is a witness. That is why they walled him up in the lime kiln.'

'Saw them?' For a moment, Rawle was unsure.

Lamb and the sergeant heaved Newton towards the door.

'Wait,' Rawle said. 'You say he saw the murder take place?'

'This a wild accusation,' Lamb said. 'Ever since I arrested his brother — '

'He saw Constable Lamb on the quay,' Newton said. 'He was there while the murder was committed.'

'Sir,' Lamb appealed to Rawle. 'This is fantasy. The boy is as deranged as his brother.'

'You stand there and tell me one of my constables witnessed a murder and did nothing?' Rawle's voice sank to a whisper.

Outside, clouds rolled up the estuary like cannon smoke; the sky darkened. There were shouts from the street below; shopkeepers lowered their blinds; coach drivers hurried their horses; passers-by called out warnings about a downpour.

'You expect me to take the word of this scrap of an orphan?' Rawle started to arrange the papers on his desk. 'Are there any other witnesses?'

'It was late,' Newton said. 'I understand the boy was the only person on the quay. Constable Lamb was there keeping watch while his father and brothers searched the boat for anything they might have missed. They found the girl hiding there; she gave them the slip on the night of the wreck. She saw them take the other women. When she refused to go with them, they slit her throat with her own knife.'

'Sir, this is slander. I cannot stand here and listen to — '

'Enough.' Rawle slammed his fist down on the desk top.

'Edward Rumsam later got hold of the knife and was arrested by your constable.' Newton carried on. 'The lad was so weak-headed he would have forgotten where he got the knife within five minutes, and so suggest-ible he would have confessed to anything he was told to.'

'Sir,' Lamb appealed to Rawle again.

'Who unlocked the cell the night the rifles disappeared? While the sergeant was with me on the quay, where were you, Constable?' Newton rounded on him. 'How were the crates transported out to the lime kiln? Was it on a cart with muffled wheels?'

'Take him to the cells.' Rawle glared at Lamb. 'Unsubstantiated allegations have no credence. However, be assured I shall interview the constable's father and brother personally. In the meantime, I shall decide what charges I can bring against you.'

Rawle nodded towards the door.

'Take him.'

* * *

Dirty light filtered in through a high, barred window. Newton spent the morning lying on the wooden bench. He had given all his intelligence to Rawle; if the superintendent chose not to investigate, there was nothing he could do. As soon as he could get out of here, he would telegram Gillis to let him know the guns were found. His duty now was to escort Abigail safely back to London. His head ached; he tried to ignore the fiery pain in his jaw; when he ran his fingers across the side of his face he couldn't tell whether the swelling had subsided.

At noon Abigail arrived, bursting with news.

'I have wired my papa. He will contact Sir Lawrence and demand your release. As soon as the superintendent receives his telegram, he will have to let you go.'

Never happier than when she was at the

centre of things, Abigail smiled confidently.

'He even had the nerve to intimate that he possessed enough evidence to charge me.' She sounded genuinely shocked. 'I demanded to know whether it is against English law for people to defend themselves.'

Abigail settled herself on the bench beside Newton and insisted he let her inspect his bruises. She turned his head one way and then the other and peered closely in the meagre light. She pulled back the collar of his shirt and ran her hands over his swollen shoulder; he could feel the kindly touch of her fingers on his skin long after she had finished her examination.

'I shall have some arnica ointment for you next time we meet.'

Newton gave her a lopsided smile.

'I have been to the vicarage; the girl is much recovered. I just wish I was able to discover her name; in the fullness of time I expect I shall.' Abigail laughed. 'Mrs Dauncy does nothing but complain that she is eating them out of house and home.'

Newton was about to say something, but Abigail wouldn't let him interrupt.

'I am taking the girls shopping in one hour's time, the one from the vicarage and the others. I intend to buy clothes and shoes for them all. I am looking forward to it. I have invited

Mrs Dauncy to accompany us and I believe she is excited too.' Before Newton could ask, she continued. 'The others are currently still at the Newfoundland Inn. Dear Lizzie has fed them and lit a fire in one of the rooms so they may take it in turns with the bath. They were half-starved, the poor wretches. They were terrified. They still will not be parted one from the other for a second.'

'You have managed the situation expertly.' Newton smiled at her.

'Sergeant Culley says boats from that part of the Irish coast often sail as far as northern Spain. Some local bandits must have kidnapped the girls and sold them to the Irish gunrunners.'

'Who then ran off and abandoned them at the first sign of trouble,' Newton added.

'It is a good thing they did.' Abigail refused to let anything darken her sunny mood. 'Or we should not have them with us now.'

'And is Culley recovered?'

'He has a large swelling on the back of his skull.' Abigail was serious. 'He wanted to come up here to try to reason with the superintendent to release you, but I persuaded him otherwise.'

'Persuaded him?' Newton sounded doubtful.

'His blurred vision is a symptom of

concussion which could result in lifelong damage if he does not allow himself sufficient time to recover. I ordered him to rest. Anyway, I told him that my father would contact Sir Lawrence.'

'And will he be . . . ?'

'Provided Sergeant Culley rests, he will recover fully in time.' Abigail looked straight at Newton. 'I assume the superintendent will bring charges against this Lamb character for attacking us.'

'He says the men were going about their business. He says they heard about the girl at the vicarage and were taking the others to reunite them. When we surprised them, they assumed we meant them harm.'

'Going about their business in the middle of the night? The superintendent means to let them get away with it?' Abigail was shocked. 'What about the girls?'

'We have no proof,' Newton said. 'Lamb claims the girls were kept under lock and key for their own protection. Rawle chooses to take the word of one of his own constables.'

'What about Norman? They walled him up in a kiln.'

'Rawle will not take Norman's word that he witnessed the murder on the quay. There is no corroboration. Constable Lamb will contradict him. Whom do you think Rawle is inclined to believe?'

'That poor boy. He is resourceful, brave and he repays kindness with kindness.' Abigail stared up at the barred window. 'Yet no one pays him attention; he is just an orphan on the quay. He deserves much better.'

'Dauncy will make sure he is sent to the workhouse.' Newton tried to offer her some consolation. 'It is probably for the best. At least he will be kept out of trouble.'

'For the moment, he will hardly leave my side.' Abigail smiled. 'I left him sitting on the step outside waiting for me.'

They looked up as the sound of the sergeant's key clattered in the lock.

'The superintendent says that's long enough, miss.' The sergeant looked sheepish; he failed to catch Newton's eye. 'We don't allow visitors as a rule.'

'Very well.' Abigail got to her feet at once. She smiled reassuringly at Newton.

'I shall buy clothes for Norman as well as the girls.' Abigail laughed at the thought of it. 'The outfit I got for him is ruined already; his cap did not last a day.'

'The stationmaster's urchin?' The sergeant tutted disapprovingly. 'Turned up again, has he? Westcott will give him what for. That boy ran off without so much as a by-your-leave.'

'I'm taking care of him now,' Abigail said

firmly. 'The boy has good qualities and will grow into a fine man one day.'

'Don't be taken in, miss.' The sergeant shook his head. 'He'll show you all the good qualities you like as long as you're spending your money on him.'

'I believe you are wrong, Sergeant,' Abigail said.

Calling out goodbye to Newton, she smiled politely at the sergeant and hurried up the stairs.

$$\star \quad \star \quad \star$$

Rawle ordered a carriage from the quay and insisted on escorting Newton to the station in time for the last train to Exeter.

'I received a telegram from Scotland Yard. My instructions are clear,' he said. 'You and Miss March are to board a train tonight.'

As they crossed the bridge, Newton took a last look back at the town. The early-evening sky was pale and empty; shadows clustered in the doorways along the quay. The first fishing boats sailed in on the evening tide. The men heaved wooden boxes of mackerel, skate and John Dory on shore, lined them up and waited for customers. Further along, there were crates of crab and lobster. Lizzie Hookway, a coat pulled over her apron and a straw hat jammed on her head, led the charge of women haggling over prices; a young woman Newton guessed must be Charlotte trailed after her with a basket in each hand.

'The Board of Guardians are sure to return the child to his mother,' Rawle said. 'It will save a tidy sum for the workhouse budget; besides, everyone knows Mrs Hookway.'

'What will happen to the *Brianna*?' Newton said.

The broken mast still dragged in the water; a pile of rigging bobbed on the current like seaweed.

'Auctioned off, if no one claims her,' Rawle said. 'The harbour master will see to it.'

On the bridge, pedestrians stood aside to let the carriage pass. As they reached East-the-Water, the shipwrights' hammering echoed from the dry dock. The coachman urged the horses up the hill towards the station yard.

'This is yours.' Rawle produced a ticket from the pocket of his uniform. 'I shan't wait. Your sergeant and Miss March will already be on the platform as well as those women.'

Newton took the ticket.

'Arrangements are being made for the yeomanry to collect the rifles. Until they get here, two of my constables will stand guard over them night and day.'

There was no need for Rawle to explain; Newton had the feeling that he was attempting some kind of apology.

'If it wasn't for your friends in high places, I'd still have you under arrest.' Rawle stared out of the carriage window as though something in the station architecture suddenly caught his attention. 'We should have found a way of working together.'

The carriage lurched over potholes in the station yard and drew to a halt.

'I understand how an accusation against one of your own men — ' Newton began.

'We are short-handed here.' Rawle didn't let him finish. 'A constable's pay is low. I know the risks in employing a man like Lamb, but he is tough and strong and literate. When I took him on, he looked as though he might have the makings of a good policeman.'

'Looked as though . . . ' Newton stared at the superintendent. His head throbbed; the bruise on the side of his face burned. 'What are you saying?'

'By the time I get back to the station Constable Lamb should have signed in for his shift. I suspect he will not turn up. I also suspect he forced his sister to leave her child with you to make you look foolish; it was an attempt to discredit you, to make it impossible for you to pursue the investigation. The father may have been behind it, who knows?' Rawle held his stare out of the carriage window for a moment longer. 'A weaker man than you, Inspector, would have taken the next train to London rather than stay on and risk a scandal. I am certain of that.'

Embarrassed by this unexpected praise, Newton was silent.

'You also know the word of the orphan will not be admissible testimony, even though what he says may be true.'

'About the murder of the girl?' Newton's brain somersaulted.

'The boy's story is no good without corroboration,' Rawle said. 'He has a reason to lie. He would like nothing better than to see Constable Lamb in trouble.'

'Then why this sudden change of heart?' Newton was genuinely perplexed.

'You know Lamb's brother fled from the lime kiln.' Rawle turned to look at him.

'Miss March's shot frightened him,' Newton said. 'He showed no loyalty to the old man.'

'Most likely they took the coast path to Cornwall,' Rawle said.

'They?' Newton said. 'Miss March repaired the old man's wound on a table at the Newfoundland Inn.'

'I sent two constables to bring him to the station just before I set out for the station with you. I wanted to question him myself.'

Then Newton understood.

'He wasn't there.' Rawle looked grave. 'On Miss March's instructions, Mrs Hookway built up the fire for him and left him in the parlour bar. When the constables arrived to fetch him he had gone.'

'You think he has made off down to Cornwall with his son?' Newton said.

'I have sent men on horseback to look for them both.'

'What about Constable Lamb?' Newton said.

'As I said,' Rawle said quietly. 'I wait to see whether he signs on for the night watch.'

On the platform, the Reverend Dauncy made it his business to oversee a red-faced Westcott and the station porter struggle to load a new-looking trunk into one of the coaches. Abigail insisted on it being placed in the passenger compartment with them rather than being consigned to the guard's van at the rear. The girls, all wearing new dresses, hats, shawls, long gloves and carrying ladylike parasols, huddled together, and kept up an animated commentary on everything.

At Abigail's insistence, Culley remained seated on a bench. He managed a smile, but his usually pale face was ashen. His movements were stiff and awkward; he was obviously still in pain. Mrs Dauncy stood beside Abigail and stepped forward to greet Newton.

Abigail took Newton by the sleeve and stood him in front of the young women. She went through the motions of introducing him. The girls giggled shyly and stared at the ground until she gave up.

'They look . . . ' Newton found that he didn't quite know what to say. 'You have had a most successful trip to the shops.'

'They loved it,' Abigail said.

'Miss March is most generous.' Mrs Dauncy beamed. 'Those girls are very lucky.'

'Mrs Dauncy and I have enjoyed ourselves.' Abigail smiled warmly. 'You should have seen the looks on the girls' faces.'

'I believe I shall miss them.' Mrs Dauncy dabbed her eye with a tiny handkerchief. 'The feeling is most unexpected.'

'We had a fashion parade at the Newfoundland Inn,' Abigail went on. 'Dear Lizzie wanted to see them in their finery. She and I said our goodbyes there; she said standing on the platform would be too much. But I have promised to write; it is the least I can do.'

The Reverend Dauncy checked the time on his pocket watch, gave an agitated little dance on the platform and turned to his wife.

'As soon as the train leaves, we must make haste, my dear,' he confided. 'I have an appointment at the vicarage. A widow wishes to discuss arrangements for a christening. She has decided to move down from London following her bereavement. She stayed one night in a hotel and then moved into lodgings in the town. She may need your assistance.'

'Of course, my dear.' Mrs Dauncy was entranced by the girls' dresses; she barely heard him. 'Don't these young ladies look a picture?'

At the end of the platform, steam exploded from beneath the engine. Westcott climbed down from the carriage. Abigail thanked him and pressed coins into his hand. As the engine's whistle shrieked, Dauncy ushered the girls into the coach.

'I expected Norman to put in an appearance.' Westcott sounded half-irritated, half-disappointed. 'You say he was with you this morning.'

'Miss March bought him a new jacket and trousers.' Mrs Dauncy scanned the platform. 'He knew the time of the train; we discussed it.'

'He's got wind of the fact the Reverend plans to dispatch him to the workhouse,' Westcott said. 'He'll have run off again.'

'The parish guardians have the best interest of orphan children at heart.' Dauncy over-heard them. 'You have done your best, Mr

Westcott, but we can't have children running wild.'

'I'll miss the little blighter,' Westcott conceded. ''Course, I'm not surprised he's taken it into his head to disappear; he don't know the meaning of the word grateful. That's something they'll learn about him at the workhouse.'

Newton took Abigail's elbow and helped her up the steps into the carriage; Culley climbed up after them and pulled the door closed.

As Abigail leaned out of the window to say goodbye, Mrs Dauncy became unexpectedly tearful and kept repeating what a wonderful morning she'd had. Beaming delightedly, Dauncy fluttered his hands at the girls in the carriage. After a final glance up and down the platform, Westcott raised a green flag. The couplings jolted; the engine lurched; fists of steam punched the air and the platform slid away.

Inside the compartment, Culley sank back into a corner seat and immediately closed his eyes. The girls whispered intently together and darted secret looks at Newton and Abigail. Once, one of them leaned across and pinched Abigail's cheek softly and threw her arms round her neck. She spoke so quickly and sweetly that the words became melody;

the meaning was lost, but the emotion was clear. Abigail laughed delightedly; a blush rose in her cheek.

The train followed the east bank of the river out of town. A convoy of fishing smacks, low in the water, sailed in on the tide. Towards the estuary mouth, on the opposite bank, a line of half-built hulls lay lined up at right angles to the water's edge; the newly sculpted wood gleamed as pale as milk in the afternoon light. The hills which rose behind the shipyard were lush and green, criss-crossed by dark hedges and dotted with sheep. The western sky carried a hint of gold, the first sign that afternoon was giving way to evening.

'Inspector.' Abigail smiled at him. 'I have something to confess.'

Newton smiled in return. Her words sounded light and playful; it was as if she were teasing him. Once he would have taken offence, but not now; the realization delighted him.

'Oh yes?' he said.

Abigail leaned down and snapped open the fastenings of the trunk. The girls stopped talking and watched her. Culley shifted in the corner and opened his eyes. Abigail threw back the lid and there, lying perfectly still on a mattress of haberdasher's parcels, wearing a new jacket and trousers with a cap folded and tucked in his pocket, was Norman. As the girls screamed, he sat bolt upright. His grin was ear to ear.

'Hello, Inspector,' he said. 'I'm going to Canada.'

# 16

*Three days later*

As Newton was shown in, Chief Inspector Gillis stood at the window and surveyed the morning traffic which blocked St James's. He was alone in the room. A coal fire warmed the air. The pages of a handwritten document were spread on a low table next to a leather armchair.

'Sir Lawrence will not be joining us; I've just had word. Can't say I'm surprised.'

He strode towards Newton and clasped his hand warmly. 'Anyway, it's good to see you, Theo.' He peered at Newton's face. 'Nasty bruise.'

'I thought Sir Lawrence called this meeting.'

'Haven't you heard?' A cynical smile played on Gillis's mouth. 'Much too busy to talk to the likes of us.'

'He wanted me to report back in person,' Newton said.

'Promoted.' Gillis shrugged. 'I sent your report on to him; I assume he read it. He's been recommended for a seat in the Lords and asked to head up an inquiry into land drainage in Lincolnshire.'

'Then his concern about a Fenian threat . . . ' Newton began. 'What's that got to do with land drainage?'

Gillis raised his eyebrows.

'Mr March?' Newton said. 'Will he be here?'

'Still in bed with bronchitis.' Gillis sniffed dismissively. 'I suppose his daughter will turn up in his place.' He stared deliberately out of the window. 'I hear you two got along rather well down in Devonshire.'

'Miss March and I . . . ' Newton felt the words dry up in his mouth. 'Yes, we did.'

Gillis chuckled. He took one of the armchairs and gestured Newton towards the other.

'I've been through your report. Now I'm halfway through reading what she said about you.' He picked up the document from the table. 'She commends the tenacity, clearheadedness and courage of the Metropolitan officers in tracking down the wrongdoers and the persistence they showed in the face of lukewarm support from the local constabulary. This is a copy of what she wrote for her father.' Gillis scanned the writing. 'There are some other things as well.' He skipped over a paragraph or two. 'Here it is. Apparently you treat unfortunate women and children with sympathy and understanding.'

'Well . . . ' Newton was caught unprepared.

'Point is,' Gillis said, 'this report has gone to the Home Office, with your name on it. You've been noticed.'

'We found the rifles,' Newton said modestly. 'It wasn't easy. Culley helped.'

'Ah yes, Sergeant Culley.' Gillis settled into his chair. 'What did you make of him?'

'Never let me down,' Newton said. 'I didn't get to know him well.'

'He's been sent back to Liverpool.'

'Already? He took a nasty bang on the head.'

'He's had a couple of days in bed. Left from Euston this morning.'

'Undercover work?' Newton said.

'I was never sure whether Culley was working for Scotland Yard, the Irish police or Sir Lawrence.' Gillis considered. 'Now Sir Lawrence is out of the picture, it looks as though someone from the Home Office has taken him on. I expect I'll hear in due course.'

'He grew up on Sir Lawrence's estate,' Newton said. 'His father was a gamekeeper. Chanced on a cache of Fenian guns and they killed him for it. Sir Lawrence looked after the family after that.'

'Adds up.' Gillis nodded.

After knocking briefly, a uniformed porter pushed the door open. He carried a note on a silver tray.

'Yes, of course.' Gillis sounded irritated. 'By the back stairs, I suppose.'

The man slid out of the room.

'Can never get used to these places,' Gillis growled. 'Too many flunkeys, notes on trays, women not allowed to use the proper staircase. Your Miss March is on her way up.'

Newton couldn't be sure, but he thought Gillis was struggling to keep a straight face. When the door opened, the men jumped to their feet. All smiles, Abigail breezed in. She shook Gillis's hand and peered at Newton's bruises.

'Looking better, Inspector.'

Newton was thrilled to see her; he knew he was blushing and could do nothing about it.

Gillis offered to ring for refreshment.

'I should have liked to stay, but they wouldn't let Norman come up with me.' Abigail sounded indignant. 'It's not enough that they make me use the back stairs, they insist he waits outside the building. The doorman even told him not to stand close to the entrance.'

'Norman?'

Gillis looked at Newton for an explanation.

'My father sends his apologies.' Abigail collected herself. 'He has asked me to pass on his thanks to you, Inspector, for providing an escort for me. He says he hopes to see you before we leave London.'

Abigail handed Newton an envelope with his name handwritten on the front. Unwilling to open it in front of Gillis, Newton slipped it into his pocket.

'I'm glad we are back safe and sound.' He nodded shyly.

Still concerned to do the right thing, Gillis asked if Abigail would like to sit down.

'If I did not have Norman to worry about, I should like to stay,' Abigail said.

'I'm sorry,' Gillis said. 'Norman?'

'I haven't included his journey to London in my report.' Newton caught Abigail's eye.

'The boy who witnessed that terrible business?' Gillis was lost. 'You brought him with you?'

'I have made arrangements for him to travel to Canada. I shall place Norman in the care of the Macpherson organization. They lodge orphans and abandoned children on farms in Ontario until they find placements for them; families adopt them and give them a proper home. Norman will become a citizen in due course. If he stayed in Devonshire, they would pack him off to the workhouse.'

'This is very good of you, Miss March.' Gillis was impressed. 'I hope the lad appreciates what you are doing for him.'

'Of course he does; he is excitement itself.' Abigail beamed. 'He delights my father with endless questions about the new country. He wants to know everything.'

'Macpherson will find him a permanent home?' Gillis said cautiously.

'On a farm, most likely. I shall make it my business to keep a check on his progress and see him from time to time provided the distance is not too great.' Abigail smiled. 'And if it is, I shall write to him.'

'And the girls?' Newton said.

'Girls?' Gillis was wide eyed. He stared at Newton. 'You brought girls back from Devonshire as well?'

'Yesterday, I hired a hansom cab; we toured the docks together,' Abigail said. 'Eventually we found someone who speaks their language, the captain of a freighter transporting iron ore from Bilbao. It turns out they are from a region of northern Spain. He is willing to take them. The captain's wife sails with him; she will look after them on the voyage.'

'They won't want to leave you.' Newton smiled at her.

'For the time being, I have found them lodgings in a shelter run by Carmelite nuns,' Abigail said. 'They are in the best hands.'

'Have you discovered how they came to be aboard that boat with the weapons?' Gillis said.

'Traded.' Abigail's face fell. 'Sold in exchange

for rifles. They were snatched from their villages by men they didn't know and locked in a house on the coast until the Irish boat came.'

'I shall arrange for an interpreter to be found and statements to be taken,' Gillis said fiercely. 'These will be passed on to the superintendent in Bideford. It will be useful when he catches those other rogues.'

'Are they still missing?' Abigail said. 'I thought the superintendent planned to arrest them on the coast road.'

'Gone to ground somewhere,' Gillis said. 'Don't worry, miss, the Borough Police will track them down.'

'Gentlemen, I am not prepared to leave Norman alone on a London street,' Abigail announced. 'And now I have delivered my father's letter . . . ' She smiled at Newton. 'I believe it contains a dinner invitation for one evening next week. He assumes he will be recovered by then.'

After Abigail had taken her leave, Newton and Gillis settled themselves in the leather chairs.

'Fine young woman,' Gillis said. 'Strong-minded. I can imagine her standing up to that ruffian in the farmyard. That urchin boy has fallen on his feet; there are boys like him on every quayside in the country.'

Newton stared into the fire and let Gillis talk. His thoughts were still about Abigail peering at his bruised face, smiling at him. In his pocket, he could feel the shape of the envelope she'd handed him.

'One thing you don't know,' Gillis went on. 'The day after you left, the story appeared in the newspapers: Irish boat bound for Liverpool wrecked on Devonshire coast; cache of Fenian weapons discovered; MP instructs Scotland Yard to investigate. It was a leak, of course. Who do you suppose was responsible?'

Gillis didn't expect an answer.

'Wasn't me, wasn't you. Had to be Sir Lawrence's office. Who else could it have been?'

An idea was forming in Newton's mind, but he couldn't yet see the full shape of it.

'Question is, why tip off the press?' Gillis went on. 'I'm surprised you didn't have reporters chasing after you on the next train.'

'He took the credit.' Newton shrugged. 'He wanted everyone to know.'

'And if that's what he fed to the newspapers, who can say what rumours he started around Whitehall?' Gillis looked pleased with his hypothesis. 'Low and behold, within forty-eight hours, he'd been promoted.' He leaned forward confidentially. 'This is just between us. Wouldn't do to let the Canadians know.'

As blue flames danced across the coals, Newton's thoughts drifted. He recalled walking the length of Bideford Bridge for the first time with Abigail keeping pace beside him. It was his first sight of the town. The houses huddled together in the lee of the hill, their casements sparkled and their limewashed walls caught the soft afternoon sunshine. Beneath swaying masts, the vessels heaved at their moorings and the incoming tide charged under the arches of the old bridge. The sky was bright; clouds raced in from the sea; overhead, gulls wheeled and dived.

'Suddenly, Sir Lawrence was the man who had uncovered a Fenian plot,' Gillis went on. 'Promotion in the bag.'

The fire crackled; tiny sparks arced between the coals.

'That's why he wanted us back.' Newton pulled himself out of his reverie. 'He telegraphed Culley more than once. He wanted us back as soon as we'd got there.'

'And why was that?' Gillis asked.

'He'd got his promotion,' Newton said quietly. 'He didn't need us to find guns or anything else. The longer we stayed down there, the more chance something might go wrong.'

'Makes me wish I was still a sergeant,' Gillis grunted. 'Arrest a few villains, crack a few skulls and make the world a better place. I used to enjoy it.'

'How did he know?' Newton asked. A light flared in his head like a gas mantle just lit. 'How did he know they were Fenian guns? How did he know the boat was bound for Liverpool? Just a guess, was it?'

Gillis's face was a mask; Newton couldn't read it.

'If you're going to be promoted,' Gillis began, 'and you will after this, you've got to know whom you're dealing with. These people, politicians, civil servants, they wrong-foot you all the time. They're all after something and you never know what it is. Give me a good, honest criminal any day.'

Newton was lost again. Gillis was telling him something and not telling him. He couldn't grasp it. He remembered the boat with the broken mast trailing alongside her, the clot of torn rigging moving like seaweed in the swell. He remembered the sight of Abigail in the water fighting against the tide. He remembered kicking off his boots ready to throw himself into the river after her.

'The boat came from a village on Sir Lawrence's estate in Ireland,' Newton said. 'Culley told me.'

'I edited your report.' Gillis's face was stone. 'I took out that part and had it recopied. If Sir Lawrence knew you'd included that, you'd be cooling your heels in some bridewell while his lawyers took months to prepare their libel suits.'

'Culley was in Liverpool.' Newton thought aloud.

Gillis nodded.

'Any sergeant from Scotland Yard could have come with me. Sir Lawrence insisted on Culley. His eyes and ears, you said.' Newton slipped another piece in place. 'If the *Brianna* had made it to Liverpool, Culley would have been there to meet it.'

'And discover the rifles.' Gillis helped him.

'But because of the storm, the boat was wrecked, the guns were discovered and the story was out. Sir Lawrence publicly picked an officer from Scotland Yard to go and collect them. Of course, he made sure Culley went along to keep an eye. Meanwhile, he leaked the story and got his promotion. After that, he didn't care that the crew had run off and the guns went missing; he wasn't interested any more.'

Newton stared at Gillis. There were words in his mouth, but he was almost afraid to say them.

'Sir Lawrence arranged for the guns to be shipped to Liverpool and arranged for Culley to discover them. He invited the Canadians so that their visit coincided. When the storm wrecked the ketch he covered himself by sending me — he couldn't very well order a sergeant down from Liverpool to conduct an investigation in Devon. Either way, it gave him the ammunition he needed to blow whatever opposition he faced in the government out of the water.'

He sat back in his chair and let the enormity of what he had just said wash over him.

'Very clever.' Gillis stretched his feet out and let the fire warm his legs. 'Without proof, though, it's just speculation.'

'There's no proof,' Newton said. 'Never will be.'

'And what about the girls?' Gillis said. 'You're not going to suggest our ambitious MP was engaged in running Spanish dolly-mops to Liverpool?'

'Culley had been in Liverpool for three months,' Newton said. 'That's far too long to wait for a boat from Ireland. Maybe he was expecting the boat sooner.'

He picked up a poker and jabbed at the coals in the grate.

'If Sir Lawrence was here, he'd ring for some flunkey to do that.' Gillis laughed. 'You're like me, you'll never make a proper gentleman.'

Newton wasn't listening.

'Sir Lawrence didn't know about the girls,' he said suddenly. 'The crew aboard the *Brianna* calculated they'd have safe passage into Liverpool because of the guns. Why not make a detour to Spain? They could buy girls from some gang down there, pay with Sir Lawrence's rifles and bring them back to Liverpool. It would be easy to find a whoremaster on the docks to sell them to; they could make up a story about some of the cargo of rifles being washed overboard. I told you there were only a few boxes. The hold could have carried much more.'

'More speculation,' Gillis said. 'No proof and not a shred of evidence. This is just two coppers chewing the fat, carping on about their superiors like coppers always do.' He looked fiercely at Newton. 'Besides, this is a private conversation, so let's keep it private.'

'Just speculation,' Newton agreed.

Gillis levered himself out of the armchair.

'Time to get back to the Yard and do some proper police work,' Gillis said. 'I get tired of all these shenanigans.'

Newton crossed to the window. Below him on the pavement, Abigail and Norman stood staring up at the building opposite; Norman was pointing at something. At first Newton thought some feature of the architecture had caught his eye. Then he saw a lone seagull swoop down, land briefly on a windowsill and stare down at them. They waited until the bird flew off.

Norman clasped Abigail's hand and smiled up at her. Newton remembered the surly, suspicious boy with his cap pulled hard down whom he met at the station only a few days before. Abigail was laughing and pointing things out; she shared his delight in observing everything that went on in the street. Newton watched them until they turned and headed off towards Piccadilly. Norman chattered on and stopped and stared whenever something caught his eye; all the time his hand gripped Abigail's.

'There is another possibility.' Gillis joined Newton at the window.

Momentarily, Newton lost sight of Abigail and Norman in the crowd; a stab of disappointment caught him unawares. A closely packed tide of people, carriages, hansom cabs and delivery carts flowed up and down the street. He searched the faces, scanned the backs of heads, waited until the traffic passed until he spotted them again; they resurfaced near the turn into Park Place. Abigail had her arm round Norman's shoulder so the crowd could not separate them.

'If your theory's right,' Gillis said, 'someone in the government could have rumbled what Sir Lawrence was up to.'

Newton still stared out of the window; he didn't want to look away while he could still see her.

'They wouldn't want anyone upsetting any apple carts.' Gillis spoke quietly, as if he was sharing a confidence. 'Wouldn't do to have fears about Fenian threats reignited now the Home Rule debates are underway, would it?'

Abigail was at the corner of Jermyn Street.

'What are you saying?' Newton turned to look at him. When he stared out of the window again, Abigail had gone.

'Suddenly promoted and given land drainage to look after?' Gillis laughed briefly. 'Sir Lawrence has been kicked upstairs. Somebody powerful has noticed what he has been up to and put him where he can't do any damage.'

Newton turned away from the window and slid the envelope from his inside pocket. Inside was a sheet of cream notepaper covered in stylish copperplate. Newton wondered if March had dictated the note and he was looking at Abigail's own hand. The letter thanked Newton for his report and for providing an escort for Abigail; it drew attention to the success of the short expedition and described how it had given him evidence to take back to his government of the threat which both countries faced.

Newton was just about to refold the notepaper, when the final paragraph caught his eye.

*As you know, Inspector, Canada is a young country; we are anxious to recruit citizens who will help us to develop into a great nation. The Dominion Police Force not only upholds the law in our cities and western provinces, but also protects our borders. It needs officers like yourself, possessed of courage, skill and experience. I should be obliged if you would consider taking a position with us. Perhaps you would be so good as to contact my daughter to arrange a date when you would be free to discuss this proposal next week over dinner with us at our hotel.*

'They've offered me a job.' Newton held out the letter for Gillis to see. 'In Canada.'

'Trying to poach my best officer, are they?' Gillis snatched it out of Newton's hand. 'Well, that's easy.' He scowled. 'Accept his invitation to dinner and turn down his offer of a job.'

Newton studied the letter again.

'I'm serious.' Gillis glared at him. 'Don't get ideas about waltzing off to the colonies. I need you here.'

Newton turned back to the window for a second. Pedestrians crowded the pavements; a hansom cab pulled up sharply and forced the traffic to a standstill; a flower-seller rushed forward as soon as a man in a black silk hat stepped down into the street. Newton slipped the letter back into his inside pocket. Aware of the warmth of the paper against his shirt, he searched the crowd for a glimpse of Abigail just in case she had turned back.

'Well?' Gillis demanded an answer. 'What will you do?'

Newton smiled. Right then and there, he knew, really knew. Abigail had shown him. It had nothing to do with what anyone expected of him; nothing to do with his career or following orders from Scotland Yard; nothing to do with etiquette or any notion of gentlemanly behaviour. Without fear or favour, he was going to expect the best and treat people as they deserved, men or women, high or low, strong or weak.

'Well?' Gillis was waiting.

'Defend the defenceless,' Newton said.

We do hope that you have enjoyed reading this large print book.

Did you know that all of our titles are available for purchase?

We publish a wide range of high quality large print books including:
**Romances, Mysteries, Classics**
**General Fiction**
**Non Fiction and Westerns**

Special interest titles available in large print are:
**The Little Oxford Dictionary**
**Music Book**
**Song Book**
**Hymn Book**
**Service Book**

Also available from us courtesy of Oxford University Press:
**Young Readers' Dictionary**
**(large print edition)**
**Young Readers' Thesaurus**
**(large print edition)**

For further information or a free brochure, please contact us at:
**Ulverscroft Large Print Books Ltd.,**
**The Green, Bradgate Road, Anstey,**
**Leicester, LE7 7FU, England.**
**Tel: (00 44) 0116 236 4325**
**Fax: (00 44) 0116 234 0205**

*Other titles published by Ulverscroft:*

# ONE BULLET TOO MANY

## Paul Bennett

Life in the Polish resort on Lake Cezar is idyllic. That is, until local crime lord Emil Provda starts a protection racket among the local businesses. But this time, Provda has picked a fight with the wrong person. Hotel owner Stanislav is a former mercenary soldier — and when his former brothers in arms hear their old comrade is in trouble, they agree to come out of retirement for one final fight. Putting their lives on the line, Johnny Silver, Red, Pieter and Bull are determined to close Provda down if it's the last thing they do . . .

# AN OXFORD TRAGEDY

## Norman Russell

1894: Sir Montague Fowler, Warden of St Michael's College, Oxford, dies from apparently natural causes. Before long, however, vicious rumours begin to circulate that he was murdered. Concerned, Captain Stanley Fitzmaurice approaches Detective Inspector Antrobus of the City Police — and an autopsy reveals that the dead man was poisoned with mercuric chloride. Who would benefit from the warden's death? His three children are all in desperate need of money . . . Meanwhile, as suspicion falls heavily upon Timothy Fowler, Dr Sophia Jex-Blake agrees to look into the matter. She and Antrobus must work together to finally unravel the truth.

# DEAD AND GONE

## Bill Kitson

Dean Wilson knows that any relationship between him and Naomi Macaulay is doomed. Her family were the founders of Bishopton Investment Group, which collapsed amidst claims of fraud and embezzlement — and he has ties to the person responsible for the crash . . . When Dean is charged with assault, DI Mike Nash's enquiries lead to him reopening the old fraud case. Then events quickly escalate to the point where he has several murder investigations on his hands . . .